BY SUN AND CANDLELIGHT

by

ELIZABETH RENIER

ace books
A Division of Charter Communications Inc.
1120 Avenue of the Americas
New York, N.Y. 10036

For

JANE VANSITTART

in appreciation of her generous help with research into conditions in eighteenth-century India

> How do I love thee? Let me count the ways.
> ...I Love thee to the level of every day's
> Most quiet need, by sun and candlelight.
>
> Elizabeth Barrett Browning

He led her to where the wood thinned; then, glancing over his shoulder, drew her in amongst the trees. Here they were hidden from the laborers working the fields below.

"Now is the moment I have been waiting for," he said, and his voice sounded strangely thick and unfamiliar. He held her wrist and stood looking down at her. His eyes had suddenly become hard and cold.

"I do not know whether you are a good actress or merely a fool," he said in a harsh tone. "Whichever you are, you must be taught a lesson."

"But why? What have I done?"

"What have you done? Why, you've cheated me, you wide-eyed, innocent-looking chit. I was led to believe you were being guarded like a princess in a tower. And what do I find? That quite openly, under your guardian's very roof, you have bestowed your favours upon another man. And now it is you, my pretty, who is going to make amends."

Other ACE BOOKS by Elizabeth Renier:

The sun was filtering between the window shutters when Phyllida Marchant woke. She stretched luxuriously, idly tracing with her forefinger the embroidered flowers of the bed curtains. The snug hollows of the feather mattress, the familiar faded blue of the canopy above her head, gave her a sense of security, assured her each morning that the world about her remained unchanged and safe.

It had not always been so. She could still recall waking in a different kind of bed, one which rocked from side to side, in a little room whose walls were not brick or stone but fashioned of plain wooden boards smelling of resin. Until that other, seemingly safe, world had been shattered.

Even now, in nightmares, she could hear her mother's screams, the savage cries of the men with painted faces and feathers in their hair; could feel herself snatched by white hands from the brown ones which held her by the heels and flashed a knife towards her throat. In a kaleidoscope of memory there was the smell of burning, the shouts of men, horses whinnying; the darkness of the wood through which she travelled on horseback, muffled in a man's heavy coat. There had followed another darkness in which the people around her, all strangers, moaned and groaned as the floor beneath them heaved and shuddered, and the walls of this strange new house rolled from side to side like her little bed. Nowhere in all this confusion was there a face she knew. Not once, although she cried and cried, was there an answering word from her mother, nor the reassurance of her father's deeper voice.

When she was old enough to understand it had all been explained to her: how her parents had been murdered by Red Indians in their isolated home in Virginia, which was one of the American colonies 3,000 miles away across the Atlantic Ocean. She herself had been saved by a detachment of King George III's soldiers, and taken to a ship about to sail for England. She had been wearing a little chain around her neck with her name and date of birth, which had enabled the kindly merchant and his wife who had cared for her on the ship to trace a relative in England—an uncle, her mother's brother. A bachelor of forty-five, immersed in politics and business, Samuel Gunter had at first disclaimed all responsibility for this orphaned five year old. But under the tearful pleas of the merchant's wife, he had relented sufficiently to install Phyllida in his country house at Chichester where, since he visited it only twice a year, she would cause him the least inconvenience.

His guardianship was kindly, if impersonal. He granted his niece a generous dress allowance, gave her handsome presents from time to time. He provided her with a life of comfort and social position. She had at her disposal a carriage, her own riding horse, and sufficient servants to supply the needs of a whole family. In return she had been instructed to render to Uncle Samuel gratitude and loyalty and complete obedience. Gratitude and loyalty she accorded him willingly. As for obedience, that had been easy too, for her guardian as yet had not ordered her to do anything in direct contradiction to her inclination. She had cajoled her nurse; the servants were her willing slaves. But these last two years, since Mathilda Henty had been given charge of her, life had not been quite so easy. At fifteen she found her freedom severely curbed. The expeditions with Kit, so harmless in her own eyes, were frowned upon by the thin-lipped governess.

She sat up in bed, hugging her knees, wondering by what means she could escape from the house on this warm July morning. For it was important that she should escape today. Uncle Samuel, travelling down from London, would arrive this evening, bringing an important guest, so he had written. A real milord, the housekeeper had announced with awe, and sent the servants scurrying about their business. The best silver and linen were to be used, the choicest wine brought up from the cellar. A boar's head had been prepared, a fat goose was ready for roasting. There were live lobsters which had caught the kitchen boy unawares, causing him to yelp with pain and the cook to be convulsed with laughter. Sweetmeats and fresh fruit and vegetables had been ordered, and no account to be taken of the cost.

To Phyllida, the impending visit of her guardian had only one significance. She would be tied to the house, with no chance of riding out alone, or meeting Kit.

At the sound of hooves and men's voices, she reached for a dressing wrapper and, folding back the shutters, opened the casement. A young groom was leading a saddle horse round the stable yard, carefully studying its action.

Phyllida leaned out and called to him. 'Harry, please to have my mare saddled in half an hour.'

The young man looked up, his face anxious. 'I've no time to accompany you today, Miss Phyllida. The master's ordered two saddle horses to be got ready for to-morrow and I'm not sure I won't have to poultice Neptune's hind fetlock. 'Tis a mite swollen to my way o' thinking, and you know how the master fusses about his horses.'

'That cannot take you all day,' she pointed out.

'I dursn't leave him, ma'am.'

She persisted. 'I do not wish you to accompany me beyond the city wall, Harry—only just until I meet Master Burrell.'

Before the groom could reply, the bedroom door opened. The governess' voice was harsh with disapproval.

'Phyllida, what does this mean? How dare you lean out of the window in your dressing wrapper, shouting to Harry as if you were a serving wench?'

Sighing, Phyllida closed the window. 'I wished to ask him to saddle my mare.'

'Then why did you not ring for Lucy to take your instructions?'

'It seemed such a tedious waste of time when I could perfectly well tell him myself.'

Miss Henty shut the door carefully behind her. She was tall, and not even the lavish table at Meadhayes could put any weight on her spare frame. She applied rouge patchily to her sallow cheeks. But nothing could put colour into her pale, expressionless eyes or disguise the prominent cheekbones and chin. In Phyllida's opinion, her governess' only saving grace was her hair, soft and warmly brown and so curly that however severe a cap she wore, there was usually a lock or two escaping.

She demanded sternly, 'Where do you think you are riding today, miss?'

Phyllida shrugged. 'I have not decided yet. Up on to the downs, perhaps.'

'With whom? You know perfectly well that I shall have no time to spare, quite apart from my dislike of riding horseback. And Harry is far too busy.'

Phyllida answered casually, 'I had thought to meet Kit.'

Miss Henty said stiffly, 'You will please to accord people their proper names.'

Phyllida folded her hands before her and said primly,

'Very well, ma'am. I had supposed I might meet Master Christopher Burrell.'

'The son of a country physician is not suitable company for a young lady in your position.'

'Kit—Master Burrell has manners as good as any gentleman's son,' Phyllida protested hotly. 'And he is a deal more intelligent, especially than those odious young men you forced me to meet last week. Ugh! They talked of nothing but shooting and coursing and hunting. I declare they smelt of the dung heap.'

'*Phyllida!*'

Realising that the chance of this last day's freedom was in the balance, Phyllida swiftly changed her tactics. She tucked her arm through the older woman's and looked up under her dark lashes.

'Dear Miss Henty, pray do not scold me any more. This evening, and during the whole time Uncle Samuel and his guest are here, I will conduct myself with the utmost decorum and modesty. You will be proud of me, and so will Uncle Samuel, I promise. Perhaps he may be so pleased with how you have instructed me that he will raise your wages. Would not that be splendid?'

Miss Henty shook her head in exasperation. 'Child, you are impossible. Of all my charges . . .'

'I am quite the worst. I know. You have told me so before. Yet I venture to believe you are fondest of me. Come, admit it, Hen dear. In return I will declare that if I had any choice of governess, I would name you every time.'

It was not true. Often, for instance, she wished that Henty were younger. She doubted if poor Mathilda had ever really been young, had ever felt the beginning of a new day as a great adventure, had ever regarded the opening of a flower, or a bird's sweet song, as marvels to be wondered at, rejoiced in.

Kit understood. Kit was not afraid of showing his en-

thusiasm, his deep regard for life. He was totally unlike
the simpering misses whose company she must endure
at sewing parties, or the horrid boys, swaggering around
the countryside with gun or cudgel, bent on killing or
maiming some weak unfortunate creature. But then, Kit
was to be a doctor like his father.

There were so many things she and Kit had in common, she reflected: their love of exploring, of watching
the cloud shadows pass across the downs, of racing their
horses over the springy turf. It pleased her to remember
they had even been born in the same month, March,
1756.

She continued her wheedling. 'I suspect you have a
headache coming on, ma'am. You should lie down behind closed shutters, the sunlight is very strong this
morning. And,' dealing, she thought, a winning card,
'you must be at your best to greet Uncle Samuel.'

Miss Henty put a hand to her forehead. 'You are right.
I think there is thunder in the air. But, Phyllida . . .'

The girl stroked the governess' arm. 'I promise to return promptly at four o'clock. If I give you my assurance
that I will not do anything of which you could really dis-
approve . . .'

'You know perfectly well that I do not approve of
these outings at all. Should they come to Mr. Gunter's
ears . . .'

'Why should they? I shall not tell him, nor will Harry.
Nobody else knows. Nobody, that is, who would be in
the least likely to report me to Uncle Samuel. If it will
ease your mind, we will visit Kit's aunt at Clavant, who
is a most respectable widow. Go and lie down, Hen dear,
and do not be anxious about me for a moment. After all,
I have come to no harm so far, have I?'

'If I allow this, I deserve to lose my post, and am very
like to do so.'

'Uncle Samuel will not find out, I promise you. Even

if he should, I shall tell him you locked me in my bedroom because I misbehaved and I escaped by the window. He could not blame you then, could he?'

Miss Henty shook her head, sighing heavily. 'Child, child, I wonder sometimes what is to become of you. Despite all my efforts, you still have this wilful streak.'

'Which I inherit from my father,' Phyllida informed her airily. 'Uncle Samúel has told me that Papa set off for America with a new wife and scarcely a hundred pounds in his pocket, despite all his family's opposition.'

'And where did it land him, and your poor mother?' the governess demanded tartly. 'When the time comes for you to marry . . .'

'You need not have a moment's anxiety on that score. I shall marry Kit and be a most dutiful wife.' Seeing Miss Henty's expression, she added hastily, 'Pray, ma'am, do not reprimand me again. It will only make your headache worse.'

To Phyllida's surprise, instead of becoming angry the governess looked at her with a strange expression. If anything could be read into those pale eyes, Phyllida would have surmised it was pity. Yet what cause could there be for pity? She knew she would meet opposition in her determination to marry Kit. But in time, when he became a doctor, when he proved himself, she would be able to persuade Uncle Samuel, she was sure. It was not as if she were his daughter. It could mean nothing to him if she did not make a good marriage. In fact, it would surely be a relief to him to have her off his hands. Such matters, however, were so far ahead that it was mere foolishness to be concerned about them now. She was but fifteen, and so was Kit. There was all the time in the world to think of marriage.

She said as much to Kit when she met him nearly an hour later just outside the city walls. His answer was not what she hoped.

'Not all the time in the world will make it possible,' he declared ruefully. 'You will never be allowed to marry me. For one thing, I have no money . . .'

'You will have, when you are trained as a physician and earn some.'

He stared glumly over his mount's head. 'If my father's patients remain as poor as at present, I shall not be able to train in London or Edinburgh. I shall be no better than a barber-surgeon.'

'I will ask Uncle Samuel to provide the money.'

'He would do no such thing. Why should he? So that his ward, the granddaughter of a peer, should marry a poor physician's son?'

She said stubbornly, 'The fact that my grandfather was a peer has no bearing on the matter. That side of my family has not taken the slightest interest in me. Besides, my father was the youngest son and therefore without a penny. That was why he went to seek his fortune in America.'

'Nevertheless,' Kit argued with equal stubborness, 'you were born into that class, and your uncle is a wealthy and influential man.'

'What of that? It means nothing to me.'

'It means everything, Phyllida. The clothes you wear, the horse you ride, the food you eat, the carriage you drive in . . .'

'I would give them all up, to marry you.'

'It is all very well to say that now. You do not understand . . .'

'Oh, you are as tedious as Henty! The fact is, you do not want to marry me.'

'Of course I do. But can't you see . . . ?'

He broke off helplessly, realising she was not prepared to listen. What she saw, in fact, was the boy who meant more to her than anybody else in the world, and always would. His brown eyes regarded her earnestly from under dark brows. His hair was unruly, as always, curling over his ears, escaping from the narrow black ribbon in the nape of his neck. Everything about him was so familiar, and so dear to her; his serviceable brown coat and breeches, the clean but much mended linen shirt; his hands, strong and square. She studied his hands as they held the reins of the sturdy cob which made her thoroughbred black mare look almost underfed by comparison. Those hands had healing in them, like his father's. She remembered when she had first noticed them, carefully holding a delicate china cup.

He had come to Meadhayes five years previously with some medicine his father had sent for the housekeeper. It was a winter's morning, bitterly cold, and Phyllida had insisted he be given hot chocolate in the little parlour. She had joined him there. At first he had been shy and silent. But when she persuaded him to talk, she had known at once that he was like no other boy she had met. For one thing, his path was clear. His schooling, and the help he gave his father, left little time for games or any other country pursuits enjoyed by other lads of his age. His mother had died when he was eight, leaving him, like herself, an only child.

Their friendship had deepened over the years. Although his free time was limited, Phyllida considered every hour spent with Kit was worth a dozen endured in the polite, dull society her governess considered more suitable. Kit had taught her Latin, persuaded her to widen her reading beyond Miss Henty's scope. He had taught her country lore, the use of herbs, how to apply a bandage or a tourniquet. All this knowledge she absorbed with eagerness, since one day it would enable her to help him in his work. For two years now she had dreamed of marriage to Kit. In the dream it was always summer and she and Kit securely happy in their present untroubled relationship which gave her so much joy.

To Kit, the relationship was no longer untroubled. He watched her as she rode ahead of him, erect and slim in her green habit. Always she chose a green riding habit. Sometimes it would be of velvet, dark as fir trees; sometimes in a lighter material, with the vivid colour of young grass. The present one was lime green, showing to perfection her black hair, her wide grey eyes and fair skin with the soft pink flush in her cheeks. She was lovely, there was no denying it. And would be lovelier still when she grew to womanhood. But she was not for him, unless a miracle occurred.

She moved in a world of luxury which was alien to him. To Kit, life meant sickness and death and poverty. For every ten accounts he made up, five would be crossed out by his father as unlikely ever to be paid. Often medicines would be provided out of his father's purse. The wife of a country doctor had few servants. She had to manage on a strict household allowance, to produce a meal at any hour. She saw little of her husband, rarely entertained. It was unlikely she would own more than one fashionable dress, and certainly she would not have her own carriage. Phyllida would be totally unprepared for such a change. Despite his attempts to explain, it all seemed perfectly simple to her. In her plan for the future her guardian would wave a magic wand and provide all the luxuries she was used to, for herself and for Kit, too. He could never make her believe she would not be allowed to marry him. If he tried, she would airily inform him that she would wait until she was twenty-one and could please herself. It was useless to point out that at twenty-one he hoped to be at one of the big hospitals. Or that, should she persist in her determination, Samuel Gunter would withhold her dowry, make quite certain she did not inherit a penny of his money. To Phyllida, her guardian was a kindly, generous man who cared for her happiness. To Kit, whose father had friends in London, another side of Samuel Gunter's character was known.

Kit urged his mount forward. 'Where are you heading for in such a hurry?'

She answered hesitantly, the colour flooding into her cheeks. 'I thought we might pay a visit to—to my house. It is a month since I have been near it.'

Exasperatedly he demanded, 'Why do you still persist in calling it *your* house?'

Her answer was defensive. 'Nobody else takes any interest in it. Even Francis Delaney's steward does not care a jot for the house or garden. His concern is solely with the estate.'

'Naturally. Since *that* brings in some money, which an empty house does not.'

'Money! How you harp on that subject. If it comes to that, what has already been spent on the house will be wasted if it is allowed to remain unlived in, uncared for, indefinitely.'

'It is likely to remain so for some years yet, while Sir Francis is in India.'

'It is strange,' she mused aloud. 'Although I know him to be quite grown up and serving with the King's army in India, I cannot think of him as other than a child, an orphan child like myself.'

They were riding side by side through a wood. She let her reins fall slackly on the mare's neck and spoke softly. 'I love to dwell on that story, of how Sir Francis's father bought the land near Clavant and had the house built as a present for his wife. She spent her childhood near Chichester, you know, and loved this part of Sussex. She was delicate and nearly died when her son was born. And so Sir Henry, to please her . . .'

'Phyllida!' Kit's voice was sharp with protest. 'You know full well it was not like that at all. It was well known that Sir Henry Delaney was a rake and a drunkard and cared not a jot for his wife's health or happiness.'

She went on speaking in the same dreamy tone as if she had not heard him. 'Sir Henry had this house built, as I said. But before Lady Sarah could come down here with her baby son, she had a seizure and died.'

'Phyllida, why will you not accept the true story? Sir Henry had this house built on the pretext of his wife's ill-health, but in reality to keep her away from London. After four attempts she had fulfilled her purpose. She had produced an heir. Sir Henry's taste was for courtesans, women of the streets. It was because of that, because he heaped every indignity upon her, that she died. You know as well as I do how she died—by throwing herself under the wheels of her husband's carriage.'

Phyllida shuddered. 'Why did you have to say that? My version is much better.'

'It is not the true one. You must keep to the truth.'

She turned wide grey eyes upon him. 'Why? What harm can it do anyone to pretend it happened my way? Moreover, if I choose to believe that Sir Henry Delaney died of a broken heart . . .'

'You are distorting the truth. He died in his cups, with a trollop on his knee.'

'You do not know that, Kit, you were not there.'

'Everyone in Chichester knows it. My father was in London at the time, the story went the round of all the coffee houses.'

Her chin lifted stubbornly. 'Nevertheless, I shall not believe it. I shall continue to make up my own story. And I hope that poor Sir Francis was never told the truth if it is as horrid as you say.'

'He was but a child at the time. I dare say they made up some fancy tale to satisfy him. But he'd learn the facts when he grew older.'

'The facts,' she repeated scornfully. 'Must you always insist on those?'

He answered patiently, 'I am to be a doctor, Phyllida. It would be useless to pretend a child had a touch of croup when it was dying of pneumonia.'

'That is quite different. When it is of no consequence whether one speaks truth or fancy . . .'

'There is no doubt you are a woman. Your mind is like this path, full of twists and turns.'

She tossed her head and retorted with dignity, 'In any case, I do not think you should speak to me of courtesans and—and trollops. It is not a fit subject to be discussed with a young lady.'

He burst out laughing. 'I do not suppose you really know the meaning of the words.'

'Of course I do.' Her retort was defiant but again she had strayed from the truth. 'They are—they are women with whom one does not mix, like shopkeepers' wives or milkmaids.'

Kit's laughter rang through the quiet wood. 'You are so innocent, Phyllida, it is scarcely credible.'

'What is wrong with that? Henty tells me there are certain facts it is not proper for me to know until I am married.'

'It is to be hoped you do not learn them, by error, long before,' Kit muttered. But when, not understanding, she asked him to explain his remark, he refused, and rode doggedly forward with what looked very like a scowl on his normally good-natured face.

Although he avoided looking at her, her image imprinted itself on his mind so that instead of the trees ahead he saw the curve of her small breasts beneath the tightly fitting habit, the graceful line of waist and thigh, the still childish mouth with its full lower lip. He grew uncomfortably hot and eased the collar of his shirt which seemed suddenly too tight. His voice sounded thick as he called over his shoulder.

'Let us canter. The horses grow restive at our slow pace.'

They emerged from the trees into open country. Away to their right the downs, patterned with white dots which were grazing sheep, were softly green against the blue sky. In the strips of fields, barley, oats and wheat swayed in the breeze. An old woman, tending a flock of geese feeding by the roadside, looked up as they passed and nodded a greeting. The track sloped downwards to where the river flowed through water meadows and a huddle of cottages formed a triangle about a village green. Beyond, half hidden by trees, was 'Lady Sarah's house'.

It had never been known by any other name, since the first brick was laid. Now, twenty years later, it still waited, silent and empty, for someone to open wide the doors and windows and let in sunshine and new life.

Phyllida rode past the great iron gates with the Delaney coat of arms in fading colours above the rusting padlock. With Kit following, she skirted the high wall and turned left where a narrow path followed the meandering course of the river. Ducking her head to avoid overhanging branches, she led the way to a small open space, hidden from both river and road, and waited for Kit to help her dismount.

Here, the solid grey wall had cracked and fallen, leaving a gap through which they had ventured many times in the past five years. Impatiently she watched him tether the horses, then took his hand and scrambled over the broken stones. Brambles and nettles came up to her waist, but the thick skirt of her habit and her leather boots protected her. Over the years she and Kit had made the semblance of a path through the wilderness of the garden, up to the house. On either side was a lush tangle of rampant growth: bushes entwined with bindweed, ivy strangling the trunks of beech trees; rose beds golden with buttercups. A flurry of small birds rose from the ornamental fountain. A jay fled screeching above their heads. The black and white of a magpie flashed against a dark conifer. The panicky escape of some small creature was marked by a stirring of the tall grass.

In contrast to the sound and movement in the garden, the house was eerily silent and dark. Shading her eyes against the sun's glare, Phyllida peered through the windows of what she assumed was intended as the drawing-room. To her physical eye there was nothing to be seen but dust, cobwebs, dark patches of damp on the walls, white flakes of plaster upon the bare boards of the floor. With her mind's eye she saw the room transformed. A richly patterned carpet covered the floor. From the ceiling hung a chandelier of cut glass and rock crystal. A Chinese lacquer cabinet held Sèvres porcelain figures and pot-pourri bowls from Dresden. In one corner there was a harpsichord; in another a lady's escritoire. It was all so clear to her. Sometimes it was as if she could hear voices and music, as shadowy figures moved about the room or sat upon the green silk and painted chairs. Sometimes she could visualise in every detail the women's full skirted gowns, the silk breeches and flowered waistcoats of the men. She could even picture their hair, the ladies' dressed high and ornamented with feathers, the gentlemen's powdered wigs. Yet not once had she been able to imagine a face. As soon as she thought to capture one feature clearly, the whole dissolved. Had it been an old house she would have believed herself seeing ghosts. But no-one had ever lived here. Only the feet of masons and carpenters and plasterers had trodden those uncarpeted floors; only the workmen's rough voices had drawn echoes from the silent rooms.

To Kit, she knew, it was just an empty house. This

fantasy of hers was one thing they did not share. Sighing, she turned away from the window, to discover that he was holding a young blackbird in his hands. She took off her glove and stroked the fledgling's downy back. Then, noticing the hen bird flying agitatedly from bush to ground, her beak full of worms, Phyllida urged Kit to put the baby down.

He did as she wished. 'It will be lucky to survive,' he remarked, 'with all the enemies that can find cover in this wilderness of a garden. It has about as much chance as a child in the hovels I visit with my father.'

She ignored his last remark. She was still thinking about the house. Life teemed in the garden, in the river flowing beside the high wall, in the very air about them. Only the house was dead. Drawing-room, bedrooms, nurseries, all were empty. No horse had stamped and whinnied in the stable, no dog barked at the approach of a carriage. No smoke had spiralled up from the chimneys. Nobody, she was sure, had ever laid a hand upon the warm brickwork and felt the loneliness of the house, its hopeful waiting. Not even Kit understood the intensity of her feeling for this place. Not even to him could she reveal that, in the privacy of her bedroom at night, she prayed that one day it might have a mistress who would love it as she loved it, and bring happiness to blot out the tragic memory of the woman for whom it was built.

Kit's voice broke into her reverie. 'We had best be going if we are to reach Aunt Phoebe's by midday.'

Phyllida gave one last look at the house, then followed him. 'How wonderful it would be,' she said dreamily, 'if you were Sir Francis Delaney and we could be married and live here happily for ever and ever.'

He was about to answer her sharply, impatient with her fancies. Then he saw her face, so young and wistful. She was but fifteen, after all, he reflected. There was time enough for her to be disillusioned, for her dreams to be shattered.

Feeling years older than her, instead of a mere two weeks, he held out his hand to help her over the jumble of stones. He wished he might always be at hand to help her over the rough places, and knew the wish impossible of fulfillment.

The storm broke when they were still half a mile from Chichester. As they emerged from the trees they were lashed with a downpour of rain so fierce that in a few minutes Phyllida's habit was saturated, her hair straggling on her shoulders. The plume on her hat trailed forlornly over the brim, her cravat was a limp rag against her neck. She dared not stop to shelter, since they were already later than she had intended. Nor could they make much speed along the rough road, pitted by heavy wagons and made slippery by the passage of cattle. It was not much better inside the city walls. The central gutter could scarcely contain the rush of water. The filth of the street eddied about their horses' legs.

Bidding a hasty farewell to Kit, Phyllida turned thankfully into the stable yard. She dismounted swiftly, tossed the reins to Samuel and ran into the house by the side door, hoping to escape detection. In the hall Miss Henty was pacing up and down, wringing her hands. At sight of Phyllida, she hurried forward.

'Child, where have you been? I sent Harry out to find you and—Oh, what a state you are in!'

'I am sorry, ma'am. We . . .'

The governess cut short her explanation. 'Up to your room, at once.' Then, at the sound of voices on the landing, she gasped in dismay.

Samuel Gunter appeared at the head of the stairs, accompanied by a stranger, a tall thin man in black, wearing a heavily curled wig. As he started down the stairs, her guardian caught sight of Phyllida. He stared at her in horrified disbelief; then turned hastily and caught hold of the stranger's arm.

'My lord,' he said in an unnaturally loud voice, 'I venture to draw your attention to this portrait of my grandfather. It is considered one of . . .'

Grabbing Phyllida's hand, Miss Henty dragged her unceremoniously along the hall, through the kitchen and up the back stairs. When they reached the girl's bedroom, the governess sank into a chair, gasping for breath.

Flinging off her dripping hat, Phyllida faced her defiantly. 'What need is there to act as if I had committed some dreadful crime? Everyone suffers a drenching at some time or another.'

'If Lord Stansted should have caught sight of you . . .'

'I dare say he would have been vastly amused.' Phyllida giggled as she peeled off her gloves. 'At least I don't have to wring out a wig. Now, if *he* were caught in a rain storm . . .'

Miss Henty rose. 'You do not understand, child. Oh, where is Lucy?' She tugged violently at the bell rope.

'What is all the hurry? It wants an hour to supper, though I declare I'm starving already.'

'Mr. Gunter gave orders that you were to be ready in ten minutes, to be presented to Lord Stansted. I did not dare tell him you were not even in the house.'

Phyllida stared at her. '*Presented?* To my uncle's guest? Such a thing has never happened before. The less he has seen of me, the better I have pleased Uncle Samuel.'

'This time it is different. This time—Oh, thank heaven, here is Lucy.' She turned to the maid. 'Now hurry, girl. And Phyllida, you are to stop asking questions and allow Lucy to dress you as quickly as she may.'

Phyllida was too wet and uncomfortable to offer any further protests. She submitted to the quick rub with a rough towel, to having her stays laced so tightly she could scarcely breathe, to the ruthless tugging at her tangled hair. The sooner she was dressed, the sooner she would eat and that need at the moment was paramount in her thoughts.

'Who is this Lord Stansted?' she asked the governess, who was observing the toilette with critical eyes.

'He is a very important acquaintance of your guardian, a gentleman of some influence in political circles and a member of the Court of Directors of the Honourable East India Company.'

'He sounds exceedingly dull and I cannot imagine why he should have the slightest desire to meet *me*.'

The governess offered no further explanation. Phyllida saw with astonishment that her maid was beginning to pile up her hair.

'I am not going to a ball,' she protested.

The maid shot a glance at Miss Henty. 'I was told to make you look your best, Miss Phyllida.'

'Oh, very well.'

Phyllida could tell by her governess' face that Miss Henty would brook no opposition. Philosophically she accepted the situation. After all, Henty had allowed her this long day out with Kit, which was taking a considerable risk on the governess' part.

She asked sweetly, 'Is your headache better, ma'am?'

'Yes. No. I have scarce had time to think about it.' She went over to the window and stared down into the street. Her voice sounded muffled, as if she had difficulty in speaking. 'Phyllida, you do realise you are entirely dependant upon your guardian? That without his protection, his provision for you, you have nothing?'

'Of course I realise it,' Phyllida answered cheerfully. 'I have always been most grateful to him.'

Miss Henty turned swiftly. 'Then you will show your gratitude by giving him unquestioning obedience?'

Phyllida was puzzled. 'Have I not always done so? I

admit I have behaved indiscreetly at times and done things of which doubtless Uncle Samuel would not entirely approve. But in all important matters . . .'

'Nothing has been of so great importance as the matter your uncle will impart to you this evening.'

Phyllida rose from the dressing stool and went across to the governess. 'What is it, Hen? Why are you so solemn?'

There was the same expression in the governess' eyes that had intrigued Phyllida earlier that day; anxious, almost pitying. Then her mouth tightened and she squared her thin shoulders.

'You will learn soon enough,' she said, and her voice was harsh. 'Now, let me look at you.'

Phyllida stood still while the governess paced slowly around her and the maid stood anxiously by. A flash of lightning lit up the western sky and Phyllida marvelled that the governess, who was usually afraid of thunderstorms, seemed oblivious of this one. Glancing into the mirror, she was surprised by her own reflection. In the pale blue gown with the tight bodice, her figure was as slim as a boy's. But the jewels at her neck and in her ears, the swept-up syle of hair, had transformed the bedraggled hoyden of fifteen minutes ago into a striking young woman. Secretly she had practised making herself look older. She had never imagined that her maid would be instructed to do so, that Henty would approve such a procedure.

The governess, with a word of approval, dismissed the maid. 'You look—very charming, my child,' she said jerkily. Leaning stiffly forward, she touched Phyllida's cheek lightly with her dry lips.

Before the girl could recover from her astonishment, the governess' manner changed. 'Come, we must not keep the gentlemen waiting any longer. And, Phyllida, pray remember all that I have taught you.'

Her guardian was waiting in the little parlour at the back of the house. Phyllida disliked this room, it was always so dark. The small windows faced east but a high wall and a cluster of tall buildings prevented the sun from ever penetrating. Miss Henty had considered it most suitable as a schoolroom since, unlike the rooms at the front of the house, it did not offer the distraction of the street to her pupil.

Uncle Samuel stood in his favourite attitude, legs firmly apart, hands clasped beneath his coat tails, the heavy folds of his chin overlapping his linen cravat. At sight of him, large and beneficent, the anxiety occasioned by Miss Henty's strange manner lessened. Phyllida sank in a deep curtsey and waited to be spoken to before she greeted him.

He turned to his guest. 'There she is, my lord. Phyllida, this gentleman is Lord Stansted who has done me the honour to travel down from London to visit us.'

Again she curtsied low. 'You are very welcome, sir,' she murmured, and hoped it was what was expected of her.

As she straightened, she found herself being closely scrutinised through a quizzing glass. The tall man in the wig passed around her, just as Henty had done. Only this was different. This examination she founnd hard to bear. It was as if he were ripping away her clothes, garment by garment, and testing the flesh underneath; as if he were estimating the weight of a beast in the market-place. She glanced appealingly at her governess. Miss Henty was staring at the floor, hands clasped before her, her mouth a tight line. Phyllida turned to Uncle Samuel. He was looking on in evident approval.

She felt the colour rising to her cheeks, the palms of her hand grow clammy. The stranger ran his hands over her shoulders, her breasts, then down her skirt, feeling the shape of her thighs. Then he encircled her waist, giving it a little squeeze. A hot flame of anger flared through her whole being. No-one in all her life had touched her in this way. She felt confused, ashamed, and quite helpless. Yet since her governess made no protest; since her guardian so obviously approved, could the experience be as shameful, as horrible, as she believed?

At last the ordeal came to an end. Lord Stansted stood before her, smiling. She did not like his smile.

'And what are your accomplishments, young woman?' he asked.

She answered abruptly. 'I can sew and embroider and paint a little. I can also read and write, even some Latin.'

'*Latin!*' Her guardian's tone betrayed his astonishment.

She saw Miss Henty's head jerk up. Then she was aware only of light glinting on the quizzing glass, close to her face.

The visitor remarked sneeringly, 'Latin indeed. To what use do you suppose you will put such an unlikely language?'

Infuriated by his behaviour, she answered recklessly, 'When I marry . . .' She saw her governess' raised hand, and faltered. 'That is, sir, I—I do not know. I find it a useful exercise for the mind.'

Her guardian's bellow of laughter gave her some slight reassurance. 'Do you hear that, my lord? You will agree she is a young woman of some originality of thought?'

The quizzing glass swung idly on its black ribbon. Lord Stansted rubbed his chin with a thin forefinger. ' 'Tis not an attribute I care for in a woman, Gunter. The younger generation of our family are not over equipped with brains. I would not do to introduce a woman who outshone them.'

'I am sure my niece would be most discreet,' Uncle Samuel remarked hastily.

Again Phyllida looked to Henty for enlightenment,

but found none. She wondered how much longer she must stand there, being cross-examined, having her qualities discussed like a slave girl in the market-place.

Her guardian glanced anxiously at his guest. 'Well, my lord, does she please you?'

Lord Stansted gave Phyllida a last appraising look and turned to his host. 'She will do well enough, I think, provided she keeps her learning to herself.'

Uncle Samuel's face lit up, the anxiety left his eyes. He smiled at Phyllida, patted her benignly on the shoulder.

'You may leave us now, child. Lord Stanstead and I have much to discuss.'

Scarcely able to conceal her relief, she curtsied briefly to both gentlemen and went swiftly to the door. Her guardian turned to the governess.

'Miss Henty, you have my permission to inform Phyllida of Lord Stansted's and my intention.'

'Very well, sir.' The words were icily polite, the curtsey no lower than was strictly required.

As they left the parlour, Phyllida heard her uncle's voice, booming with pleasure. 'I am delighted, my lord, positively delighted, that you find my little niece to your liking. She is a dutiful girl, and . . .'

His guest's thinner tones cut across his words. 'What is to my liking, Gunter, is that her hips are broad enough for successful breeding. We have no wish for another Lady Sarah in the family.'

Phyllida could hardly contain herself until they were out of earshot. Then she faced her governess.

'What is it all about, Hen? Why is Lord Stansted so interested in me? What is going to happen?' She clutched at the older woman's arm. 'Tell me, ma'am, please. I—I am grown suddenly afraid.'

Miss Henty did not allow herself to unbend. Her answer came tonelessly, without emotion. 'Your uncle and Lord Stansted are about to sign your marriage contract.'

Phyllida gripped the governess' arm until she winced. 'What did you say?'

'You heard me perfectly.'

'But—but my marriage! You cannot mean—to that odious man? Uncle Samuel would never do such a thing, he could not. Say it is not true. It cannot be true!' Desperately she shook Miss Henty's arm.

'No, no, child, not to Lord Stansted. You are to marry his nephew and heir, Sir Francis Delaney.'

'Delaney?' She repeated the name incredulously. 'You mean—Lady Sarah's son? The young man who owns the empty house at Clavant?'

'That is he.'

'Why should I marry him? I have never even seen him.'

'That is nothing unusual. From now on, you will consider yourself betrothed to Sir Francis although it is not likely you will meet for several years, since he is serving with the army in India.'

She still could not believe it. 'The whole thing is ridiculous. Betrothed to a man I have never even spoken to, whom I may not meet for years. In any case, it is impossible,' she added defiantly, 'since I intend to marry Kit—Christopher.'

Then she remembered Kit's own words, spoken only that morning. 'You know it is impossible for us to marry.' She had grown cross and argued with him. Yet in her heart she had been afraid that what he said might be true. Despite his warnings, she had allowed herself to dream. The dream now was ended.

She walked slowly up the stairs, head bent in thought. If it had to come, if she were to be forced into a marriage in which she had no say . . . And why should she have, she asked herself with a bitterness which was unfamiliar? She was an orphan and penniless. Uncle Samuel had taken her in, and he a bachelor, which could not have been easy for him. It was not for her to argue, to show unwilling. The necessity for obedience, which had been so instilled into her all these years, was being put now to the test. And after all, she reminded herself, he was doing well for her, he was marrying her into a titled family.

Sir Francis Delaney. Lady Sarah's son, the owner of Lady Sarah's house, 'her' house. She paused, a hand gripping the stair rail. So one day it would be hers, in reality. She would be the one to open wide the doors and windows, to choose the furnishings, bring life into the empty shell. And Francis Delaney himself? How often in the past had she imagined herself meeting him, the central figure of a tragic story, comforting him, making him believe her version of how his parents died instead of the sordid truth. But he was a grown man now. She reckoned it up. He must be twenty-two. With a commission in His Majesty's army, serving with the East India Company of which his uncle was a director. He would be in no need of comfort now. And what else had she to offer him, when they met? Her life compared to his was narrow and confined. Would he not find her dull?

And how would she find him? She had never even seen a portrait of him and no-one of her acquaintance had met him, since he had never been to Chichester. What, in any case, did it matter, since he was not Kit? She went on up the stairs, Miss Henty at her heels. The rain drummed against her bedroom windows, the sky was the same colour as the slate roof of the house across the street. Water gushed down the street gutter, bearing straw and leaves, a scrap of soiled linen, a dead cat. She felt the governess' hands rest lightly upon her shoulders.

'My child, it will not be for at least two years. I will

do all I can to prepare you, to help you in the time of waiting.'

Phyllida lifted her head and looked steadily into her companion's eyes. 'I know you will, Hen dear. And I shall insist that you come with me after—after I am married. That is,' she finished lamely, 'if I am allowed any say in the matter.' She caught at Miss Henty's arms and laid her head on the governess' shoulder. 'You have done your work well, Hen. You have stamped out most of the rebel in me, that same streak which sent my father to America in face of all opposition. But my father was a man and over twenty-one. For a girl, at fifteen, there is no alternative but to obey. Is there?'

The governess' voice sounded thin, choked. 'None at all, my child. None at all.'

II

Edward Glenister rode slowly down the hill towards Chichester. He slouched in the saddle, the reins loose on his horse's neck. His black boots were covered with a film of chalk disturbed by the animal's hooves. Both he and the horse were sweating in the August heat, and flies buzzed maddeningly around them.

After India, he scarcely noticed the discomfort. Madras could offer temperatures which seemed ten times higher, and as for flies, they settled everywhere in a solid crawling mass. He should have been thankful for the contrast; for the gentle slope of the downs over which the sheep grazed, for the shimmer of the sea through the heat haze, the scattered farms and cottages from which wood smoke drifted up into the pale blue sky. He should have been thankful, relieved, even perhaps a little excited at being back in England after thirteen years in the East. Instead, he semed perpetually gripped by the torpor which India and the long, weary months of the voyage home had produced. In time, perhaps, it would lift. For the present his body felt sapped of all energy, his mind of all interest.

Save for the bleating of sheep and a host of larks singing, it was quiet up here on the downs. The horse plodded on, slipping now and again on the loose stones of the track. In the past six weeks the willing beast had carried him into six countries and now at last they were nearing journey's end—if it was the end. Edward had completed his round of visits, to his parents, his brother and two sisters, married now with families of their own. Dutifully he had praised the appearance of nephews and nieces, suffered Emma to be spoiled, recounted time and again his experiences.

But always there would come the awkward moment when one of them would say, 'We were so sorry, Edward, about Ellen. It must have been quite dreadful for you.'

He had answered, 'Yes, it was,' and known himself a hypocrite. Not that he had wished her dead; only to be free of her, free of the whining voice, the incessant complaints, the determined negation of her attitude to India. Of course it had all been his fault in the first place. There were women who could stand up to the conditions, and women who couldn't. And Ellen couldn't, had never even tried. He should have realised that, by the very substance of her letters over the years they had corresponded. It had been madness to invite a woman known only through the written word to come out and marry him. He had known it the moment they met and because he had known it he had felt guilty. He had gone on feeling guilty as her hatred of India increased, her health suffered; as she lost all interest in her appearance and the social activities by which other wives made life tolerable. Most of all, he had felt guilty about Emma. Ellen had not wanted a child. During the two terrible days of her labour she had cursed him. It had been a week before she would even look at the baby.

It was because of Emma that he had returned to England. He was not going to be responsible for Emma's death, as he had been for Ellen's. His resignation had not pleased the directors of the East India Company. But what did he care for them? Especially, since being in England, he had heard what some of them had done to Lord Clive. Clive, without whom there would not now be an East India Company. They had arraigned him before the House of Commons, accusing him of making an illegal fortune. They had raked up details of presents he had received quite openly sixteen years previously, taking no account of the gifts he had refused during that last residence in India, the huge sums of money, the jewels offered him by the princes. No man had adhered more strictly to the covenant forbidding servants of the Company to accept gifts from the Indians than Clive himself. He had enforced that covenant, as Edward knew to his cost, and the order ending the participation in private inland trading. That had meant there was no longer the chance to make the great fortunes of earlier years. The era of the nabobs was over. Not that he himself had ever coveted immense wealth. He had done well enough, and now, out of the blue, the chance had occured to exchange assets in India for more tangible ones in England.

The men who so jealously, so ungratefully, put Clive on trial, had lost their case. But they still held their positions. That greedy power-seeking merchant, Samuel Gunter, for instance, and his crony Lord Stansted. Edward ground his teeth. He knew what he would like to do with men like that. Take them from their cosy London coffee houses, their cool drawing-rooms, their safe all-powerful niche in Leadenhall Street and put them down in the Indian jungle amongst the wild beasts and the fevers, the treacherous enemies whom you thought were friends; set them to face an Indian army thousands strong, a barrage of artillery or a charge of trained elephants, as Clive had done. Clive's achievements had been beyond what could be expected of any man, especially in that damned, inescapable heat. And now, it was said, his health was quite broken and his brave spirit bruised beyond healing by the attack upon his honour—an attack instigated by men who knew not the meaning of the word.

The horse's ears pricked forward, he jerked up his head. Edward tightened his hold on the reins, hearing hooves in the distance. Somebody was riding, he thought ruefully, with a deal more energy than himself, for the unseen animal sounded to be galloping at full stretch.

Below him, a wavering ribbon of dust rose above a hedge, marking the rider's progress. He watched it hanging in the air away to the left. Then his interest died and he sunk again into the dark thoughts which seemed as inescapable as his own shadow. His mount jerked up its head again, ears forward. Edward could see nothing to account for its sudden nervousness. It went down the slope reluctantly, rounded a corner; then shied so violently he was all but unseated.

The cause of its fright, he saw with astonishment, was a woman in a green riding habit, sitting on a bank in the sparse shade of a clump of hawthorns. Her hat with its sweeping feathers lay beside her and her black hair was tumbled about her shoulders. As she rose and came towards him, he saw that she was young and very pretty. No, not pretty, he amended. Handsome, in a wild, rebellious fashion. Her face was flushed. There was a trace of blood on the full lower lip, and her forehead was streaked with dirt. The knuckles of the small hand clutching her whip gleamed whitely.

'Heaven be praised!' she exclaimed, when he had brought his mount to a standstill. 'I had thought to be marooned here for hours.'

Edward raised his hat. 'Your horse has bolted, ma'am?'

She scowled at him. 'Naturally. You do not suppose I was sitting on that wretched bank for pleasure, surely? I have already walked for miles, it seems, after that stupid creature, Centaur, and all because of a hare no bigger than a mouse. He almost leapt over the hedge in fright, and threw me headlong.'

'You are not hurt, ma'am?' Edward asked anxiously.

'I have sustained nothing worse than a few bruises and stings from the nettle patch in which I landed. Why are you dismounting?'

'To give you what aid I can.'

'Surely your obvious course is to retrieve my mount. He is over there, beside the wood, or was when I last caught sight of him. I will wait here, in the shade.'

He stared openly at her, taken aback. By heaven, she might be merely a slip of a girl but she had more spirit than many a man he'd had under his command in India. If Ellen had possessed even a jot of such spirit . . . Abruptly he checked his thoughts and concentrated on the immediate present.

'As you wish, ma'am.' He reached for his hip flask. 'Allow me to offer you some wine to refresh you while you wait.'

She took the flask from him and sniffed at its contents. Then she looked up and smiled. The quality of her smile was like Emma's, innocent and trusting, surprising him into a pleasure he had thought long past.

It took him half an hour to catch her mount, a young, nervous chestnut. But at last he rode triumphantly along the track with the quieted animal trotting beside him. When he came to the clump of hawthorns he thought for a moment that the girl had wandered away in search of him.

Then he saw her. She was lying on the grass at the foot of the bank, her eyes closed, one hand clutching the flask. Hurriedly Edward dismounted. Tethering the horses, he knelt beside her, fearing that despite her assurance she had been injured by her toss. She was breathing quite naturally. Her cheeks were still flushed, her lips a healthy pink. Her breasts, youthfully rounded beneath the tight-fitting green habit, rose and fell gently; her dark lashes lay like a child's on the soft cheeks. There was a mole like a beauty patch just above her mouth.

Edward laid his hat on the grass and knelt on the dusty track, uncertain whether to rouse her or let her rest awhile. Suddenly, the sense of pleasure stirred in him again. And something more, much more: desire, which he had learned to vanquish as if it were a mortal enemy, so many times had Ellen rejected him. Like the treacherous enemies he had known in India, it came upon him now, powerful, taking him unawares. He clenched his hands against the temptation to kiss this unknown girl, not gently on her white forehead or pink cheeks, but full upon that young and wilful mouth.

Abruptly he rose. He walked a few paces along the track and stood staring down over the haze-shrouded countryside. He found that he was trembling, but not with fever. At least, not fever of the kind he knew only too well. So this was what happened when you denied emotions which were normal, natural. It was like damming a river. When the dam broke, the water rushed through, overwhelming everything in its path. If he had succumbed to that incredible desire, and she had wakened . . . To calm himself he began to speculate as to what would have happened. Like as not, instead of swooning, she would have cut him across the face with her whip. Moreover, since he assumed she lived locally, she would doubtless have spread his unwarrantable behaviour abroad so that he would scarce have dared show his face in Chichester.

He was smiling at this thought when he heard a long-drawn-out groan. Turning, he found that she was sitting up, her head in her hands. As he approached, she looked up at him between spread fingers.

She said jerkily, 'I fear I drank too much of your wine, and in this heat . . .'

He knelt beside her, his feelings now rigidly under control. 'Stay quietly for a little. I have caught your horse. In my opinion he is not a suitable mount for a young lady, especially when unaccompanied.' He added reflectively, 'I was not aware that it was the custom now in England for young ladies to ride without an escort.'

The girl said airily, 'Oh, Henty believes I have Harry with me.' Then she explained carefully. 'Miss Henty is my governess. Harry is the groom. I escape, whenever I am able.'

He eyed her speculatively. For an assignation, with some young man she was forbidden to meet?

As if aware of his reaction, she said, frowning, 'I like to be free. I like to ride or walk alone, without someone constantly watchful at my elbow.'

She seemed suddenly to realise her situation. She pressed her hands to her flushed cheeks, her grey eyes widening in dismay. Rising swiftly to her feet, before Edward could offer her his hand, she caught up her hat, brushed down her skirt.

'Indeed, sir, you must think my behaviour most unseemly.'

He said reassuringly, 'I think it is perfectly natural under the circumstances. You had a shock, you were a little . . .'

'Churlish, I fear, when first you appeared. For that I

ask your pardon. It was so great a relief to see some-body—anybody . . . Oh dear, I am making matters worse.' She adopted an attitude of primness so obviously out of character that Edward had difficulty in stifling his laughter. 'Sir, I am most grateful to you for retrieving Centaur, and for your wine. And now, if you please . . .'

'I will assist you to mount, and, with your permission, accompany you home.'

She looked alarmed. 'Oh, no. At least, not all the way. You—you are a stranger, and if I were seen . . .'

'You may rely on my discretion, ma'am,' he assured her gravely.

'Thank you. You are very kind.' She was making an attempt to tidy her hair. 'Tell me, please, do I appear very dishevelled?'

'If you will allow me . . .'

He took out his handkerchief and gently wiped away the streaks of dirt from her face. Like a child, she suffered him to do it, standing quite still before him, her face upraised, smiling a little. His desire now was to protect, not to possess. Tenderness towards a woman was now as unfamiliar to him as passion, and equally surprised him.

His voice was harsh in the effort not to betray his emotions. 'Now I will bring your horse.'

It was as he was about to mount that he noticed the button. Gold, with an engraved crest, it lay gleaming on the grass. He stooped and picked it up, recognising it as matching the ones which fastened the jacket of the green velvet habit. He was about to hand it to the girl. Then, seeing she was not looking his way, he changed his mind. He slipped it instead into his pocket.

She waited for him. As he drew level, she remarked thoughtfully, 'You spoke just now, sir, as if you were new to England. Yet you are English, I surmise?'

'I have been abroad for many years, in India.'

'India?' Her eyes lit up. 'Oh, then you must know . . . But then, I forget, India is a very large country, is it not?'

'Very large. You have a relative there, perhaps?'

'No. Well, yes, in a way. But I do not suppose . . .'

'What is this gentleman's name? Or perhaps it is a lady?'

'A gentleman. He holds a commission in the King's army. Were you also serving in that army?'

'No, ma'm. I served the East India Company in other ways. But naturally I have met many officers, both in the King's and the Company's army. What is this gentleman's name?'

'Delaney. Captain Delaney.'

He drew in his breath sharply. 'Sir Francis Delaney, heir to Lord Stansted, who is a director of the Company?'

'That is he. Then you do know him?'

Edward turned from her eager eyes and cleared his throat. His answer was cautious. 'I—I have met him on one or two occasions.'

'He is well?'

'He was, when last I saw him, some eleven months ago.'

'That is a long time.' She sounded disappointed.

Glancing at her, he wondered how near the relationship was. They were cousins, perhaps. He said guardedly, 'The passage from India is a long one, even in favourable circumstances. The ship I sailed on was old and we had many setbacks.'

'But you carried mail?'

'Naturally. Every ship does that.'

At once he saw his mistake as her mouth tightened and she looked away from him. He said hastily, 'It is quite possible that your . . . relative, had no opportunity to send a letter by this ship.'

She gave a little shrug. 'Yes, of course. In any case, I do not think Sir Francis likes writing letters.'

His mind registered the formal 'Sir Francis.' Had Delaney been cousin to her, surely she would have referred to him as 'Frank' or at least by Christian name only? Was it possible that they were not related, that the connection was not a family one? Yet Delaney had been in India for five years and this girl was no more than eighteen, he guessed.

She was fidgeting with the thong of her whip. She kept her head bent as she asked, 'Is he—Captain Delaney—as handsome as he appears in his portrait?'

'You have not met him?' he blurted out in surprise.

She raised wide eyes to his face. 'Oh no. I was . . .'

Her words were lost to him in the sudden clatter of a pheasant's panicky rush for cover. Her horse reared, plunged sideways, almost unseating her again. Edward grabbed her reins. Again he quietened the trembling animal.

'This is no mount for you,' he said sternly. 'He has been badly broken in.'

'That is why I chose him,' she remarked airily. 'I have no use for staid creatures which amble sedately around the countryside.'

'If you are not careful he will break your neck.'

'It is a risk I am prepared to take. He means no harm. I shall teach him better manners in time, when he realises I shall not beat him every time he misbehaves.'

'At least you have that amount of sense.'

She glanced at him beneath dark lashes. 'You sound very fierce, sir, as if you were used to putting young ladies in their place.'

'I have two younger sisters, though they have long gone their own way.'

'What are they called? And what, pray, is your name?'

Suddenly she laughed, a lovely sound like the tinkling of a stream. 'If dear Hen could see me now . . .'

'Hen?'

'Miss Henty, my governess.'

'She would be duly shocked, I have no doubt. But, since you have already committed the indiscretion of riding alone, I fail to see any other course open to you but to accept the help of a stranger, and his escort home.'

She nodded gravely. 'That was most sensibly put, sir. But may I not know to whom I am indebted?'

Smiling, he raised his hat and bowed to her. 'A little late, madam, allow me to present myself. Edward Glenister, at your service.'

Imitating his manner, she inclined her head towards him. 'And I am Phyllida Marchant. You look much younger when you laugh, Mr. Glenister.'

'Do I look so very old when I do not?'

She cocked her head on one side. 'You are perhaps— thirty-five?'

'I am twenty-eight,' he informed her with some asperity.

'You have perhaps been ill,' she suggested kindly.

'No. At least, not of late. It is the climate in the East which ages a man. That—and circumstances.'

She hung her head. 'I have offended you. Henty is always admonishing me for letting my tongue run away with me. I beg your pardon.'

Again he was touched by her air of extreme youth. 'It is no matter. You were merely being honest. Perhaps my return to England will improve my looks.'

'I did not say you were ugly, sir. In fact,' she added ingenuously, 'I think you quite handsome in an unusual way.'

'Unusual?'

'Yes. Because your skin is so very dark and your hair

so fair. That would be the effect of much sun, doubtless? But your eyes . . .'

'My eyes?' he prompted as she hesitated.

'They, and the lines at the corners of your mouth, are what make you look older. Your eyes, if you will forgive me, have a weary expression, rather sad, in fact.'

So, young though she was, she had recognised that. He was, however, in no mood to enlighten her. He asked abruptly, 'Is that the spire of Chichester Cathedral?'

'Indeed it is, a landmark for miles around. You are a stranger to this part of Sussex?'

'To all of Sussex. Perhaps you could recommend a hostelry where I can put up for a few days?'

'The Dolphin and Anchor,' she answered at once. 'It is quite the best.'

He was ridiculously pleased that she had without hesitation suggested the best inn, in spite of his travel-stained appearance, his lack of manservant. There was a lark singing high above their heads. Barley and oats formed golden strips between the irrigation ditches. Along the edge of the track the grass was decked out with brightly coloured flowers. He supposed it had been so throughout his long ride, but he had not noticed.

They rode through a small copse and when they emerged, the city walls showed grey and solid through the heat haze.

The girl asked, 'Are you travelling far, Mr. Glenister?'

With the habit acquired in the East, he answered guardedly, 'My plans are uncertain as yet. I have some business to transact in Chichester.'

'For the East India Company?' she asked in surprise.

'No, for myself.'

'Forgive me. I had thought for a moment you might be seeking my uncle.' The colour crept into her cheeks. 'I ask too many questions, do I not? I do not mean to appear unduly inquisitive, but you are so—so different from the gentlemen of my acquaintance. I find most of them so very dull, except Kit, of course. But, then, he insists he is not a gentleman.'

'May I ask, who is Kit?'

'Christopher Burrell. He is apprenticed to his father, a surgeon in the town. Kit is the same age as myself, eighteen. We have been friends for years. In fact, at one time I believed . . .' She broke off, shrugging. 'Did you ever have a guardian, Mr. Glenister?'

'No, Miss Marchant. My parents are still alive.'

'Are they?' Her astonishment was evident in her voice. 'Oh, I beg your pardon.'

He could not help teasing her. 'Even were I the thirty-five you thought me, it would not make them so very ancient.'

The colour deepened in her cheeks. 'I have no doubt you think me very foolish, sir.'

'I think you very charming. And I would hazard a guess that . . .'

'What? Please tell me,' she pleaded as he hesitated.

'That no-one as yet has betrayed your trust in them. I would like to believe that no-one ever will, that you may keep your delightful air of—of innocence.'

'Oh, that again,' she exclaimed impatiently. 'Kit is always telling me how very innocent I am. Yet I have read a great deal, and not only novels from the lending library. I can read and write Latin. I know a great deal about the efficacy of herbs. In fact,' she added defiantly, 'I have a great deal more knowledge than is usually taught in the schoolroom.'

Sadly he shook his head. 'Knowledge gained from books is not knowledge of life.'

'How very grave you sound.'

'I am sorry. Do not look so troubled, little Miss Phyllida. Doubtless you will make a love match and live most happily with husband and family, with nothing more than the children's whooping cough to disturb the even tempo of your days.'

'Oh, as to that . . .' She frowned and became silent, staring straight ahead. Her face had grown suddenly older. 'As to my marriage . . . Oh look, there is Kit, riding towards us.'

Edward saw a young man in serviceable brown coat and breeches, his brown hair straggling from its ribbon beneath his plain tricorne. As the rider neared them, the girl drew rein and stretched out her hand.

'Kit, how good it is to see you. Allow me to present . . .'

The young man cut her short. 'Forgive me, Phyllida, I must not stop. There has been an accident at Gallows Farm. One of the children . . .'

'Then of course I must not detain you. Is there any way in which I may help?'

'Thank you, no. There are women there aplenty,' he called over his shoulder as he rode on.

She watched him out of sight. It seemed to Edward that she had forgotten his presence.

'A very well-set-up young man,' he remarked.

Sighing, she turned back to him. 'The trouble is, he has always so many important things to do. Sometimes I am able to give him and Dr. Burrell a little help. But my guardian does not approve.'

'Of your helping him, or of the young man himself?'

'Of neither. Uncle Samuel does not think that my association wth Kit, or helping to prepare potions and bandages, is seemly for a young woman in my position. And so I have to . . .' She broke off as she saw a carriage ahead. 'Sir, I must ask you to leave me now. Once inside the gates, I am like to meet those who delight in reporting they had seen me with an unknown escort.'

He raised his hat. 'As you wish. I should greatly regret causing you any embarrassment.'

She held out her hand. 'You have been very kind, Mr. Glenister. I hope your business will be transacted successfully, that you will enjoy your stay in Chichester. I—I would invite you to call, but . . .'

'Naturally, it is out of the question. I fully understand, though I could wish our acquaintance were not so short-lived.'

She smiled at him as he pressed her hand. 'We may meet by chance.'

From any other woman he would have judged it an invitation, as blatant as a dropped handkerchief. But there was the ingenuousness of a child in her grey eyes and her smile was devoid of any provocation.

He said gravely, 'I should consider it a most happy chance, Miss Marchant. Take care when next you ride that feckless animal, or you may be left for hours sitting in a patch of nettles.'

Her laughter bubbled out. Then, as she withdrew her hand she frowned. 'Oh look, I have lost a button from my sleeve.'

For a moment he hesitated. Then he said lightly, 'A pity, but the loss is slight weighed against the injury you might well have sustained.'

Her smile broke out again, reminding him of intermittent sunshine. 'You are right. And it can be easily replaced. Good-day, Mr. Glenister, and again my grateful thanks.'

He watched her as she rode away from him, the chestnut tugging at the reins, eager for its stable and fodder. Her green habit showed clearly against the grey wall of the city. At the gate she turned and raised her hand. Then she was gone.

It seemed to Edward that the sun had totally disappeared behind a cloud. No longer was the lark singing or the flowers bright. By the time he reached the inn, which he found to be on one of the main streets, right under the shadow of the cathedral, he wanted nothing so much as a glass of ale for his parched throat, a soft bed for his aching limbs. He called for an ostler to see to his horse, and entered the inn. He was conscious of stilled voices, of barely concealed stares. Thankfully he discovered he could have a room to himself, though at first he was well aware that his appearance had excited some doubt. But when he offered to pay in advance, the doubt had quickly disappeared. He avoided answering the casual questions of the innkeeper, and went heavily up the stairs. In the bedroom he flung off his coat, tugged off his boots and sprawled on the bed. He would not stir again this day, he told himself. Tomorrow would be soon enough to call on the notary, to view his property. For now, he would lie in comfort and listen to the city noises, and think about Phyllida Marchant. It was years since he had thought about a woman in this way, recalling her smile, her wide grey eyes, that provocative lower lip. Her every gesture, every inflection of her voice seemed imprinted on his mind. He remembered ruefully her unflattering guess at his age, the kindness with which she had suggested he might have been ill, as if she were speaking to a man as old as the guardian to whom she had referred. Those questions about Delaney; he was relieved she had not pursued them. What, he wondered, was her interest in a man she admitted she had never met. A youthful infatuation with his portrait?

He yawned and closed his eyes, but the problem niggled at his mind. Then, relieved, he remembered something else, her obvious joy at the meeting with the doctor's son, the eager warmth with which she spoke of him. There, of course, was where her heart lay, the call of youth to youth. Perhaps, then, the questions about Delaney had not been on her own behalf at all. She had been vague enough about the relationship. She had probably been trying, in a roundabout way, to gain information for some friend whom Delaney had left lovesick on his departure for India. He hoped that was the explanation. For if Sir Francis Delaney should ever come within reach of that enchanting innocence . . .

He opened his eyes and frowned up at the ceiling, remembering how near he himself had come to succumbing to temptation, up there on the downs. But he had drawn back, schooled by the years of rigorous discipline of living with Ellen. Francis Delaney, so far as he could judge, had never withstood any temptation, of whatever nature, in the whole of his life.

III

To Phyllida, her betrothal to Francis Delaney seemed unreal. True, she had been given a small portrait of him, painted when he was seventeen; had received two letters from India. The portrait showed a young man of medium height with curling chestnut hair and bright blue eyes. He had been painted in conventional attitude, leaning negligently against a tree, one silk-clad leg crossed over the other; one hand, emerging from lace flounces, laid upon the head of a spaniel which gazed devotedly into its master's face. She had studied this painting long and earnestly, trying to equate what she saw with the boy whose tragic story had aroused her pity, and with the man she would one day marry.

She made up conversations between herself and this stranger to whom her life would be tied as soon as he returned to England. She practised entering a room with assured dignity, curtseying gracefully in a full-skirted gown, smiling with just the right blend of welcome and reserve. After three years such rehearsals had become tedious. In any case she had a suspicion that when the actual meeting did take place, she would simply put her hand in his, smile warmly and say, 'It is good to see you,' just as she would have done with Kit. For Francis Delaney was an orphan like herself. He had been brought up by an uncle as guardian, as she had. Would he not therefore understand the difficulties, the loneliness, of being an only child? Had he not, perhaps, weaved fantasies, dreamed dreams? She had no means of knowing, for his letters, which lay between sachets of lavender, were brief and formal, telling her nothing of himself. 'I am no hand at letter writing,' he had admitted, which had disappointed her, for there had been a certain fascination about receiving letters from an unknown betrothed so far away from England.

After Lord Stansted's departure, she had sought to question Uncle Samuel as to why Sir Francis had been chosen as her future husband. But he had been evasive, telling her that she should be proud and grateful for the excellent match he had achieved. She had been unable to gain any more satisfactory answer from Henty. Her dowry would be of a generous portion, she had been told, and since she had shown so great an interest in Sir Francis's house near Clavant, it would be put in good repair and made ready for occupation. She and her husband could spend the first few months of their marriage there, until Sir Francis decided where he wished to make his permanent home, which Uncle Samuel had no doubt would be in London. Of when he would return from India she had no idea. Some young women, she had heard, undertook the long and hazardous journey out to India to marry there. That had never been suggested to her, for which she was profoundly thankful.

If only Mr. Glenister had been able to give her definite news. Instead, he had seemed strangely reluctant to speak of Captain Delaney. There was the possibility that she might meet him again and be able to question

him further. The local grapevine of gossip had informed
her through her maid Lucy, that he was still at the
Dolphin and Anchor, that he appeared to have ample
means although he had no servant or carriage and no
baggage but what he carried in his staddle-bags. He
had been observed to pay two visits to a notary in the
town, and yesterday he had ridden out by the north
gate and taken the Winchester road. He had returned
in the evening, as sparing of information as when he had
arrived.

How much easier it was to be a man, Phyllida mused,
looking out of the window to see if there was any chance
of the rain clouds clearing. Men were not bound by
dictums of modesty and propriety. Since her betrothal,
her unaccompanied expeditions had been achieved sur-
reptitiously when her governess' headaches caused her
to keep to her room. When such opportunities arose,
she sent a note to Kit and, if he were free to meet her,
joined him at the tumbledown cottage on the track up
to the downs. No longer did he go with her to 'Lady
Sarah's house'. When she went there now, it was openly,
as its future mistress. With Harry accompanying her, she
rode in between the great iron gates of which Sir Francis's steward had given her the key. She had been inside
the house several times, enjoying to the full her new
position in contrast to the days when she had peered
wistfully through a grimy window-pane. She longed to
have the decorations started, to be choosing curtains
and carpets and furniture, to set gardeners to work in
the wilderness outside. But she had no authority to do
any of these things. They must all wait until Sir Francis
returned. All she could do was to make little sketches
and long lists which she showed to Kit. He listened
patiently to her schemes but she knew that only half
his attention was with them. He was becoming increasingly absorbed in medicine. Inevitably the future would

mean a parting of their ways, but it seemed no nearer now than it had done three years ago. Meanwhile, there was the present and it was as well to make the best of it.

Since the friend Phyllida had been due to visit this August afternoon had been taken suddenly ill, she had some hours ahead of her to fill. Seeing the sky brightening in the west, she decided to spend them visiting once more her future home. Obtaining the governess' permission, she called for her chestnut to be saddled and Harry to accompany her.

The ruts in the road were full of water and she drew up the skirt of her habit as far as she dared to avoid being splashed. She saw the young groom's interested eyes and frowned at him. There was a great deal about men that she did not understand even yet. Henty, who was a spinster, refused to enlighten her and Lucy, though obviously willing, said it was more than she dared do, for the governess had threatened her with instant dismissal if she so much as uttered a word to Phyllida on such an indelicate subject. Sometimes she was tempted to question the young women of her acquaintance, especially when she found them giggling together in a tight little group, but in the end pride stopped her. She was not going to betray her ignorance to those foolish simpering misses who fluttered their eyelashes and made play with their fans whenever gentlemen, however dull, were present. There was not one with whom she wished for a close friendship. Only with Kit was she really at ease. Yet not even with him could she discuss the strange disquieting feelings she experienced nowadays, a kind of restless longing for she knew not what; an awareness of her body which was new and a little frightening.

She rode down the sloping track to Clavant, Harry a few paces behind. Sunlight slanted from between the vanishing clouds, gilded the harvest fields, shone on the wet roof slates of 'Lady Sarah's house'. As always, her heartbeats quickened at sight of it, and she urged Centaur into a trot.

Impatiently she waited for Harry to unlock the gates, then rode slowly up the drive, savouring the fragrance of the overgrown garden. Bidding Harry walk the horses, she reached into her pocket for the key of the front door. This she always insisted on opening for herself.

Inside the house, it was dark and chill. Overgrown trees and shrubs excluded light from the downstairs windows. She walked slowly through all the rooms, playing her old game of furnishing, filling them with people. Herself, and Francis. Who else? That was no clearer than it had ever been. She tried to imagine Francis as he would be now. His hair would still be chestnut unless he wore a wig; his eyes very blue. But his skin, the fair skin of the portrait? Would that be bronzed like Mr. Glenister's? Would his face have such lines of weariness? Of course not, he was but twenty-five, whereas Mr. Glenister . . . Was twenty-eight, she reminded herself, and not the thirty-five she had guessed him. But perhaps he had been in India much longer than Francis.

Shrugging off the unpleasant thought that her future husband could age in the same manner, she looped up her skirt and mounted the curving staircase and lost herself again in her dreams. Here on the right would be her bedroom, with Francis's across the landing. Behind each, the main guest rooms; on the floor above, the nurseries and servants' quarters. It was difficult to imagine herself with children at her skirts, she had no experience of them at all. With distaste she recalled Lord Stansted's remarks about her hips. Kit had explained the facts of birth to her, quite simply, long ago, when she had been troubled by the whimpering of a terrier bitch having a litter of puppies in the stable at Meadhayes. But she did not consider it a subject to be bandied about by strangers. Nor was she a brood mare to have her points discussed.

She was in one of the upper rooms when she heard hooves clatter loudly on the gravel of the drive. She supposed it was Centaur, proving restive as ever. A few moments later, to her surprise, she heard the front door open, then heavy footsteps cross the hall. She went to the banister and leaned over, imagining it was Harry. She was about to call down and ask him what he wanted, when a shaft of sunlight broke through the branches of an elm and shone full upon the man in the hall. It was not Harry, nor Sir Francis's steward who was short and fat. This man, she could see even from her foreshortened angle, was tall. She saw also, as he took off his hat and tossed it on to the carved falcon at the foot of the staircase, that his hair was very fair. His actions showed no trace of stealth. Yet surely he had no right to be here. He moved out of the sunlight, across the hall and into the drawing-room.

Phyllida went quietly to the front of the house and looked out of the window. Harry was nowhere to be seen, but a horse she did not recognise was tethered near the fountain. She caught up her skirt and crept down the stairs. From the lower landing, by leaning cautiously over the banister, she could just see into the drawing-room. The intruder, dressed in grey breeches and a cinnamon-coloured coat, passed momentarily across her line of vision. She caught her breath, stifled an exclamation of astonishment. The man was Edward Glenister.

For a moment she hesitated. Then, assuring herself she had nothing to fear, she went resolutely down the stairs. At the doorway of the drawing-room she paused. It was evident he had not heard her. Head down, he was methodically pacing across the room, counting aloud.

Boldly Phyllida demanded, 'May I ask, sir, what you

are doing in this house?'

He swung round, hazel eyes widening. His look of surprise changed swiftly to pleasure. Completely unabashed, he came towards her, hand outstretched.

'Miss Marchant, what an unexpected pleasure to meet you again. I had no idea there was anyone else here.'

'That was obvious, Mr. Glenister,' she said tartly. 'I ask again, what are you doing here?'

He answered readily enough. 'Why, pacing out the floor.'

'To what purpose?'

'To obtain measurements for a carpet.'

'A carpet! But why should you . . . ?' She steadied her voice. 'Mr. Glenister, by whose orders did you enter this house?'

His eyes widened again, his eyebrows were raised. 'By nobody's orders.'

'Then you have no right to be here.'

His mouth tightened, he frowned. 'On the contrary, ma'am, I have every right. The house is mine.'

She took a step backward, drawing in her breath. 'Oh! How can you stand there and tell such an untruth? It belongs to Sir Francis Delaney.'

He said evenly, 'It did belong to him. Now, I repeat, it is mine.'

Unbelieving, she stared at him. He shrugged and added, 'If you still doubt me, Miss Marchant, I assure you I can produce the title deeds. And Mr. Bradley, a notary in Chichester probably well known to you, would confirm my ownership.'

She walked with short, jerky steps to the window. In the garden a magpie was chattering loudly, a sound reflecting the agitation of her thoughts.

'Do you mean that—that Sir Francis sold it to you?'

'Let us say that I acquired it.'

She swung round. 'In what manner?'

'In payment for a debt. Captain Delaney was temporarily without credit. He chose to settle in kind.'

She demanded incredulously, 'Do you mean that he made over to you, the whole estate?'

He frowned again and his voice had entirely lost any warmth. 'I know of no reason why I should be cross-examined by you, ma'am. But yes, the house and whole estate. It is a most productive one, I understand.'

She turned away. The magpie was still chattering, above a chorus of nervous piping from smaller birds. 'One for sorrow . . .'

Mr. Glenister came to stand beside her, looking down into her face. 'You appear distressed. May I now ask, what *you* are doing here, and how you gained access? Ah, I remember now. You enquired of me regarding Delaney, and yet had never met him. Is it that you have some connection with this house and were curious about its owner—its former owner?'

She took a deep breath, holding fast to the remnants of pride. His words offered a loophole from the necessity to explain, to lay bare before him the humiliation she was suffering. That this could have happened, and she not have been told . . . It was almost beyond belief, beyond bearing.

She said in a rush, 'The house has attracted me ever since I was a child. There is a place where the boundary wall is broken, beside the river. Kit and I used to crawl through. Why, I . . .' She made a wild gesture with her arm. 'I even used to picture this room as it would be, were the house lived in, were I . . .' She broke off, the colour flooding into her cheeks, a treacherous pricking behind her eyelids.

He said gravely, 'I see. And I have upset your picture? Perhaps you even peopled the house with imaginary men and women, saw them dancing in this room, even heard the strains of music, very faint?'

She gazed at him in surprise. 'How do you know that?'

He smiled, and the warmth was back in his voice. 'There was a ruined castle near where I lived as a boy. To me it was full of knights in armour. On moonlit nights I would have sworn I heard the sentry's footsteps, the creaking of the drawbridge, the jangle of harness, accoutrements. I regret having disturbed your dreams, Miss Marchant. Pray come to the house whenever you wish, but not through the hole in the wall. I will give you a key to use—that is, until I am actually living here.' His brows came together. 'This is strange,' he remarked reflectively. 'The gates were open when I arrived, the front door unlocked. How did you get in, Miss Marchant?'

Her cheeks grew even hotter. She answered swiftly, the lie coming easily. 'A relative of Captain Delaney's let me have some keys. He—he knew how very fond I was of the house, that I would not do any harm. You—you had better have them, Mr. Glenister.'

She reached into her pocket and drew out the key of the house. *Her* house, as she had thought of it in dreams, and later in reality. She stared down at the cold, hard metal and wondered how Francis could have been so cruel. For she had confessed to him by letter her attachment to the house built for his mother.

Edward Glenister's fingers closed over hers, cupped the key inside. 'Keep it, while the place is empty.' His face brightened. He struck his clenched fist into his palm. 'I have a splendid notion, Miss Marchant. You shall help me to furnish the house.'

She could have laughed aloud, bitterly. Instead, she asked, 'But—your wife?'

The eagerness left his eyes, his mouth tightened. 'I have no wife—now.'

'I am sorry. She—died?'

'Of the cholera, in Madras. She was not strong, she

should never have gone to India. I realised that, too late. I was at fault for asking her to join me there.'

She thought, with sudden perception, that is what has etched those lines about his mouth. 'You intend to live here alone?' she asked.

He gave her a twisted smile. 'Not quite alone. I have a daughter, Emma. She is six years old.'

'Poor little girl,' Phyllida exclaimed impulsively. 'My mother died when I was five, and my father. They were killed by Red Indians in America.'

'Poor little Miss Phyllida,' he murmured. 'But you were saved and brought to England?'

'The soldiers rescued me. I live now with—in my uncle's house, under his protection.'

He traced a pattern in the dust of the window-sill. 'My mother wished to take Emma, and either of my sisters would have done so. But . . .' His finger hesitated, then drew a swift, straight line. 'I wished to retain something from my marriage.' He looked up and his harsh expression lightened. 'Besides, she is an entertaining child. At least, I think so.'

'And you will bring her here—to "Lady Sarah's house"?'

To the house which seemed fated not to have a mistress, she added to herself. But he would marry again, naturally. There were sufficient single women in Chichester of suitable age and family to give him wide enough choice. In fact, his coming would doubtless cause a flutter amongst the spinsters and younger widows. For he was a man of property and evident means, and undoubtedly handsome in that strikingly unusual way.

She realised that he had spoken and she had not heard what he said. He repeated his question. 'Why do you call it "Lady Sarah's house"?'

'It is the only name it has ever had. Lady Sarah was

Captain Delaney's mother.'

'I see. Then it will not do now, I think. You must help me think of another.'

That, finally, would be the end of her dreams, she reflected bitterly. A new owner, a new name, and she herself admitted by invitation of a stranger.

Mr. Glenister raised his head at the sound of hooves on the driveway. 'Someone is coming, Miss Marchant. I fear I compromise you by talking to you here, alone. You are very young, and . . .'

'It will be my uncle's groom. Harry knows well enough when to keep silent.'

She saw his raised eyebrows, the quizzical look he gave her. Flushing, she added hurricdly, 'I mean, there are times when I meet Kit—he is the young man we encountered on our way into Chichester after you rescued me. He is a childhood friend, there is nothing . . .'

As she faltered in her explanation, he put a hand over hers reassuringly. 'Little Miss Phyllida, there is no need to distress yourself. I have not the slightest doubt that your behaviour is above reproach. But this is the second occasion on which we have met in somewhat unusual circumstances. The next time, I think, it should be a more formal affair, for your sake. If I have your permission, I will find some way of being presented to you in the proper manner.'

His words, his attitude, made her feel about ten years old. Her cheeks burned. She wanted to make some furious retort. But the shock he had given her, the dreadful disappointment which she was striving so desperately to keep beneath the surface of her mind until she was alone, were suddenly too much for her. She dared not trust herself to speak. With a little sobbing cry, she pulled her hand from his and fled from the room. She was aware of Harry's started face as she sprang up the steps of the mounting block and flung herself into the saddle. She dug her heels into Centaur's flank and went down the drive and out of the gates at a breakneck gallop. And never slowed until she was in the wood, out of sight of the house, and of the man who had just shattered her dreams.

She went at once to Kit. Surrounded by medical books and his father's fearsome instruments, he was hard at work in the study of the doctor's house in South Street. He rose as she entered, and took her outstretched hands.

'Phyllida, whatever is the matter? You look distraught. Come, sit down, let me get you a glass of wine.'

'No. No, wait, Kit. I must tell you. Something dreadful has happened. I do not know how I can bear it.'

He pressed her gently into the worn leather chair and knelt beside her, chafing her hands. 'Some ill has befallen your guardian, or Miss Henty?'

'No. It—it is "Lady Sarah's house". I am not to have it, after all.'

Kit listened patiently while she told him what had occurred. When she had finished, he fetched wine and biscuits.

'Are you sure this man is not an impostor?' he asked. 'The whole thing may well be a fabrication of lies.'

She shook her head forlornly. 'Mr. Glenister said I could enquire of his notary, that he could produce the title deeds. Oh, Kit, how do you suppose Sir Francis could have incurred a debt large enough to be forced to assign his house and estate in payment?'

Kit walked over to the window and stared into the busy street. There were many ways men incurred debts, particularly men of Sir Francis Delaney's class. Phyllida would not know of them. During his visit to London the previous year, his own eyes had been opened to the manner in which much of society lived. It was very different from the quiet respectability of a cathedral city.

And Francis Delaney had been brought up in London, under the care of his uncle, Lord Stansted, a man of whom Kit had heard a number of unsavoury tales.

Again he experienced the frustration of his association with this girl who was out of his reach. He could neither have her for his wife nor prevent her marriage to a man she had not seen and of whom she knew nothing. Even now, when the dream with which she had solaced herself for three years, the dream of living in that neglected house which had always so fascinated her, had been shattered, he could do nothing to help her.

'What kind of man is Mr. Glenister?' he asked, parrying her question about Delaney. 'I have heard he keeps much to himself and talks little.'

'You saw him,' she reminded Kit, 'the day there was that accident at Gallows Farm.'

'Only for a moment. He looked like a man who might have heavy problems.'

'He is not happy, I think. His wife died in India and he is left with a little daughter. He is not as old as he looks, he told me he is twenty-eight.'

Kit echoed her thoughts of an hour before. 'A widower, twenty-eight, and a man of property. That will set Chichester by the ears.' Trying to bring a smile to her woeful face, he added, ' 'Tis a pity you are betrothed already. Since you are first in the field you might have acquired a husband, daughter and "Lady Sarah's house" into the bargain.'

Her reaction was not what he hoped. She thumped the arm of her chair with a clenched fist. 'Do not jest. He nigh broke my heart with his disclosure.'

He looked down at her, his head on one side. 'Women should break their hearts over men, Phyllida, not over houses.'

'Do you think I did not do so, three years ago, when I knew I could not marry you?'

'You were only a child. You still are.'

'You seem to forget I am the same age as you.'

'I am a man,' he pointed out infuriatingly, 'and my life so different from yours. You are sheltered from all hardships . . .'

'I visit the alms houses, set aside part of my allowance for the poor, the sick.'

'That is true enough. Yet you are not really involved, Phyllida. No, do not argue. I am not blaming you. But when you say your heart is broken and wonder how you may bear the loss of this house of dreams, it is not really true.'

'You and your insistence on the truth!' she exclaimed in exasperation. 'Perhaps it is as well I am not to marry you, for you would drive me to distraction with your exactitude.'

'Those are fine words,' he said, laughing. 'Who taught them to you? Not Henty, surely?'

'You, I suppose. As you have taught me much that I would never have learned in the schoolroom.' Frowning, she drained her wine. 'Kit, I grow more anxious as time passes, as to what manner of man my future husband may be. Do you remember I told you what that odious man, Lord Stansted, said about my learning, that the men of his family were little blessed with brains and I would do well to forget all save a dutiful wife's accomplishments? Captain Delaney's letters would seem to bear him out. And if he runs himself into debt in this irresponsible manner . . . I had intended to enquire further of Mr. Glenister on that point, but he gave me so great a shock . . .'

'Does he know Delaney well?'

'He said he had met him only once or twice. Is it not strange, in that case, that he lent Sir Francis so large a sum?'

'Perhaps he did not lend it.'

Her eyes widened. 'What can you mean? How else could it be a debt?'

'I learned in London that gentlemen stake a great deal at the gaming tables.'

'Kit!' She clutched at his arm. 'You cannot suggest . . .'

He shrugged. 'It is a possibility.'

Horrified, she asked, 'You believe that Sir Francis could have staked our future home and the whole of his estate on the turn of a card, the throw of a dice? Oh Kit, I do not want to hear any more. I came to you for comfort. . . .'

'What comfort can I give you?' he demanded angrily. 'I am powerless. You know that. I have no position, no money save what I may earn as a doctor when, if ever, I am qualified. It is best you accept things as they are.'

She looked sadly up into his flushed face. 'If you truly loved me . . .'

'I do love you, Phyllida. You know that, too. But we are both eighteen. We cannot defy your guardian and my father—even the law itself. Even if we did, we could not live on love alone. I would do anything to help you, anything in my power. But in the end, it is so little.'

She hurried from the doctor's house as she had hurried from the manor. She did not care if her visit had been observed, reported. In fact, she would have welcomed punishment, the harsher the better, to give her the excuse for tears.

A note arrived for her next morning, brought by a servant from the inn. The handwriting was bold and clear.

At the Dolphin and Anchor,
Chichester
1st September 1774

Madam,

Yesterday evening I received a visit from Mr. Christopher Burrell who conveyed to me certain information which has greatly disturbed me and caused me no little concern on your behalf. Although I cannot claim any mutual acquaintance save Mr. Burrell, I beg leave to call upon you at any hour suitable to yourself, when I shall welcome the opportunity to express my regret that a certain transaction in which I was involved while in India would seem to affect your future happiness.

I am, Madam,

Your obedient servant,

Edward Glenister

Phyllida read the letter through several times, then went in search of her governess. Although Mr. Glenister had, she realised, done his best to cover the indiscretion of her two encounters with him, she knew she could not pretend in front of Henty, who knew her so well, that he was a complete stranger. In any case, Henty would be sure to ask why Kit should have called upon this unknown man at the inn. It would all have come out and she would have been even further humiliated before Mr. Glenister. It was better to confess.

The governess both looked and spoke her disapproval. Phyllida endured silently, 'Then I suppose I may not allow Mr. Glenister to call?'

'Oh, he had better come. But you are not to see him alone. Sometimes, child, I tremble to think what may happen to you. I have only to suffer one of my headaches and the moment my bedroom door is closed . . .'

'There is no real harm in my behaviour, ma'am, truly. You know how hard I find it to be shut up with an embroidery frame for hours. And I do so love to ride alone, to feel free, even for a little while.' She put her hand on the governess' sleeve and looked pleadingly up into the lined face. 'It is the only way in which I have disobeyed you, Hen. And when Sir Francis returns from India there will be little time left . . .'

Miss Henty was not to be coaxed into easy forgiveness. She said sternly, 'You may send a note to say you will receive this gentleman. Afterwards, I shall decide your punishment for these latest escapades.'

He came at noon, dressed in the grey breeches and cinnamon coat he had worn the previous day. His face looked drawn and there were bluish shadows beneath his eyes. When the footman had withdrawn, he said formally, 'Miss Marchant, it is indeed good of you to receive a stranger . . .'

'My governess is aware of what has occurred,' she broke in. 'There is no need for you to—to protect me, Mr. Glenister, although it is kind of you.'

He glanced at Miss Henty, his eyebrows raised. 'In that case, I will come straight to the purpose of my visit. Your friend, Mr. Burrell, informed me that you are betrothed to Sir Francis Delaney.'

'That is so.'

'And that it was your earnest desire to live at the manor house at Clavant.'

'That also is true.' She could not meet his eyes, but nervously pleated a fold in her skirt.

'Then I must express the deepest regret that circumstances have ended that hope. May I ask if Captain Delaney was made aware of your wishes in this respect?'

'Oh yes. I wrote him about it a long time ago.'

The footman brought hot chocolate and biscuits. While they were served, the visitor confined himself to some general remarks about the difference in climate between India and England. As soon as William had gone, he returned to the subject of Phyllida's marriage.

'You mentioned, I believe, that you have never met your future husband?'

'I have but seen his portrait, painted when he was seventeen. Why are you asking these questions, sir?'

He broke a biscuit, then stared thoughtfully at the pieces on his plate. 'Mr. Burrell told me that your marriage was arranged between your guardian and Lord Stansted, to whom Delaney is heir, three years ago. That would have been about the time when your guardian, who I have learned is Mr. Samuel Gunter, became a member of the Court of Directors of the East India Company?'

The governess' chocolate spilled into her saucer. 'Sir, forgive me, but I cannot think that these matters are . . .'

'My concern? Perhaps not. However, I assure you there is a reason for what may appear to you as idle curiosity. Am I correct in the assumption I have just made?'

Miss Henty's mouth tightened. 'Quite correct, sir. Miss Marchant's betrothal and the realisation of Mr. Gunter's ambition occurred at almost the same time.'

Phyllida looked from one to the other. She had not the least idea what lay behind this conversation but there seemed some peculiar understanding between this stranger and her governess.

She said sharply, 'Mr. Glenister, may I now ask you a question?'

'Certainly. It is, I can see, a habit of yours.'

She would have suspected it to be a jibe, except that he was smiling. She said carefully, 'You told me that Captain Delaney did not sell you "Lady Sarah's house" but that you acquired it in payment for a debt. How was that debt incurred?'

The change was immediate. His mouth tightened, the warmth left his eyes. Deliberately he put down his cup and saucer. 'I am sorry, Miss Marchant. That is a matter between Captain Delaney and myself.'

His refusal to answer confirmed her suspicions that

Kit was right. 'You won it from him gambling,' she burst out. 'How could you? You are older than Sir Francis. You had been in India longer. He was left an orphan, under the most tragic circumstances, as a very small child. He needed protection, not to be cheated and . . .'

'*Phyllida!*'

She threw off Miss Henty's restraining hand. She demanded again, 'How could you?'

Edward Glenister looked at her, a long, considering look which held, it seemed to her, a hint of sadness. When he spoke his voice was quiet. He appeared in no way offended by her outburst.

'Miss Marchant, your loyalty does you much credit, especially since it is on behalf of a man whom you have never met. I have no intention of defending myself against the accusations you make. You must choose to believe what you will. But I would ask you to remember one thing, that Sir Francis Delaney is no longer a child, nor even seventeen.'

'What am I to infer from that?' His very calmness provoked her further.

'I venture to suggest that 'a gentleman holding the rank of Captain in the King's army is hardly likely to relish being "protected" as you put it. In fact, Miss Marchant, for your own sake I would point out that your future husband is a man of the world, experienced in all its ways, while you . . .'

'Well?' She rose and stood before him, chin up, lower lip thrust out, her grey eyes darkening.

He looked up at her. Although he was smiling, his eyes again held that oddly sad, almost pitying expression.

'While you, little Miss Phyllida,' he said, getting to his feet, 'are scarcely more than a child, and live in a quiet cathedral city. And your knowledge of men is derived, I surmise, from your uncle who is rarely here and young

Burrell. And he, I am sure, is an upright, honest, hard-working young man and devoted to you.'

Her anger faded at his praise of Kit. She bent her head, but was still aware of his gaze upon her.

He asked gently, 'He is the one you really wish to marry?'

She caught sight of her governess' outstretched, warning hand. Ignoring it, she raised her head and looked straight at her visitor.

'Yes, he is the one. You must think that a dreadful admission, when I am betrothed to someone else. But I am dependant upon my guardian and most grateful to him for his care of me. I shall therefore obey him in the matter of my marriage as in all things. Moreover, I shall give my loyalty and duty to Captain Delaney as—as is fitting for a wife.'

He shook his head and now there could be no doubt of the pity in his hazel eyes. 'Delaney for a husband, Samuel Gunter for a guardian,' he said almost to himself. 'If ever disillusion faced a woman . . .' He shrugged and turned away, picking up his hat. 'Indeed I am sorry, Miss Marchant, to have added to your many disappointments. May I hope that, when I am installed in the manor, you will derive some small pleasure from visiting the house, with Miss Henty naturally? Emma, I know, would be most happy to meet you.'

She forced herself to be polite, to thank him. The fact remained, however, that he was inviting her to a house which she still considered hers by right, a house he had won on the turn of a card or the throw of a dice. Nothing, she told herself, would make her believe other than that he had forced Francis into such an irresponsible action.

Deep in thought, Edward walked down North Street. The crowd at the Market Cross jostled him but he scarcely noticed. He paused at the entrance to the hostelry and glanced across at the Cathedral. Was that where the wedding would take place? The wedding which should never be allowed. He could picture her so easily; the dark hair and grey eyes, the mouth whose childishness was offset by that wilful lower lip. She would be dressed all in white and never, he thought, would it be more fitting. Not for years had he encountered a young woman so innocent and free from guile or provocation or affected mannerisms. But then, he reflected, the young women who had come out to India during his time there, if they were not already married, had been openly in search of husbands.

And beside that unsuspecting girl at the altar, Delaney, whose looks and practised charm not even India had dimmed . . . And what of that other, in Madras? What would be left for her? Suttee? The accepted, even welcome, burning alive of a women who had lost her man.

He shrugged and turned into the inn. It was not his affair. He had enough problems of his own. Emma, for instance. He supposed that in time he ought to marry again, for her sake. In any case he must find a governess now he was in England, and a housekeeper and a parlour-maid and a groom. There was a carriage to buy, and all the affairs of the manor house to settle. The manor house. 'Lady Sarah's house'. *Her* house, as she had believed it.

In his room, he slumped into a chair, feeling unutterably weary. This morning he had wakened with a headache and a suspicion of fever. Most likely he was in for another bout of malaria.

He pulled his travelling chess-board from his saddlebag and set up the pieces, as he had done so many times when he was perplexed, faced with a decision. Not that there was any decision to be made, he told himself. It was not his affair, as the governess had wanted to point out. He had only to keep silent, to remain uninvolved, and nobody would be any the wiser. After all, to set himself up against Gunter *and* Delaney required more energy, more purpose than he felt capable of. Thirteen years of India, and the daily hopelessness of his marriage to Ellen, had drained him dry. Wasn't he entitled now to some peace?

Peace? At twenty-eight? He might as well be twice the thirty-five Phyllida had believed him, if that was to be his mode of thought. Angrily he swept the pieces off the board and frowned down at the empty squares. In any case, what peace would there be if he were to stand silently by, knowing what he knew, while that girl was married off to Delaney? Even if no one else ever learned the truth, it would be there always, in his conscience.

He picked up a White Queen, twirling the piece thoughtfully between finger and thumb. Then deliberately he placed it on the board.

'Queen Phyllida,' he murmured. 'What shall we make young Burrell? A King? No, a black knight, I think.' He set that piece down on the opposite side of the board. 'And you two,' he added, selecting two black castles, 'shall represent Delaney and Samuel Gunter.' These he placed in the centre. 'And myself? A bishop, assuredly, in accordance with the weight of years I feel at present. Besides, it makes my moves less restricted. Now, let us start play, forgetting all the rules.'

He moved the bishop forward and picked up one of the black castles, speaking to the chess piece as if it were alive. 'I got you out of a pretty scrape, out there in Madras. But this time, I'm not on your side. So, Captain Sir Francis Delaney, you'll have to be removed from this particular game. And I assure you, Dasim Ali and I know enough to make sure you are, with the help of the Reverend Mr. Wilkinson.'

He dropped the piece with a clatter into its box. The next move was to get the knight forward. Edward sat with his chin in his hands for some time. Then, straightening, he struck his clenched fist into his palm.

'I have it,' he exclaimed aloud.

He went across to the little table where his writing materials were set out and dipped his pen into the inkhorn.

My dear Sister, he wrote. *When I was staying with you recently you informed me that your father-in-law is an eminent surgeon greatly interested in teaching students at the hospital. There is a young man in this town in whom I am interested. His name is Christopher Burrell and I should be most grateful . . .*

His pen moved swiftly over the paper. When he had finished he sealed the letter and rang for a servant.

'The mail coach to London—when does it call?' he asked the man who answered his summons.

'Tomorrow, sir, with any luck.'

'Good. See that this goes on it. And bring me a bottle of claret.' If, as he was now increasingly certain by the tightness around his forehead, the dryness of his throat, he was about to succumb to malaria, he had better be prepared.

He bent again over the chess-board and moved the knight forward. 'Now,' he said to the castle which was Samuel Gunter. 'What about you? How do we eliminate Miss Phyllida's guardian? A powerful gentleman you are, and ruthless. It will give me the greatest pleasure to thwart you, in return for the ill you have done to Lord Clive. But it will not be easy.'

He sat frowning at the pieces which seemed now so alive to him. His head was throbbing. He was finding it increasingly difficult to concentrate. At last he shrugged impatiently.

'We will leave you to fate, I think.' With thumb and forefinger he flicked the black castle from the board. 'You'll be got rid of, though I know not how at present. And now, my two young lovers . . .' He placed them side by side, the white Queen and black knight, and picked up the bishop. 'And you, my friend, can fade quietly from the picture.' He held the little piece in the palm of his hand and slowly from his pocket drew the gold button from Phyllida Marchant's riding habit, and laid it beside the bishop. 'For you, there's this.'

He sighed heavily, then again spoke aloud. 'You're a fool, Edward Glenister. With a slight change of play, you could have her for yourself.'

He stood up abruptly, knocking over the stool on which the board lay. Such thoughts were best stifled at once, before they encouraged temptation. He'd broken one woman's spirit, he or India. It was all the same since it was because of him that Ellen had gone to that death-dealing country. Perhaps this was his chance to atone. To give another woman happiness, with no thought of any for himself.

He shivered, although his body felt on fire. When the servant brought the claret, he drank down two glasses straight off, and ordered a hot brick to be brought.

'Wait,' he ordered as the man was about to leave. 'There was a young man called on me yesterday, Christopher Burrell. Do you know where he lives?'

'Yes, sir, not far away, in South Street.'

'Then send for him. And if he knows of a better cure for malaria than a bottle of claret, tell him to bring it to me without delay.'

He flung off his clothes and climbed wearily into bed. The clock on the Market Cross chimed two and it felt as if the hammers were beating inside his head. And then he heard something else: Phyllida Marchant's voice saying, 'You are perhaps—thirty-five?' And then kindly, when he corrected her, 'You have perhaps been ill?'

Thank heaven she could not see him now, with the fever upon him. Though what would it matter, he asked himself bitterly. There was only one rôle for him to play in her life. And that role was not of a lover.

IV

On the way to spend the afternoon with an acquaintance who lived in the country, Phyllida halted the carriage at the top of the slope leading down to Clavant village. Beside her, Miss Henty, jerked awake from her doze, asked querulously, 'Why have we stopped?'

Leaning from the window, Phyllida answered over her shoulder. 'I am told there is much activity at "Lady Sarah's house." I wanted to see for myself.'

'You will see little from up here.'

'We can scarcely peer in at the gates, can we? Oh, if you knew how wretchedly I feel at no longer being able to enter that place!'

'Mr. Glenister kindly said you might visit the house at any time.'

'What joy would that give me? To see my house taken over by a man who won it through a lucky chance.'

'You do not know that to be true,' the governess remonstrated.

Phyllida turned from the window. 'Of course it is true. He did not deny it.'

Miss Henty asked reasonably, 'Have you considered that even should it be true, your future husband would have stood to gain a great deal of money had the luck gone the other way?'

Phyllida stared at her companion. 'I believe you are

positively excusing him—both of them. I think it monstrous that gentlemen should gamble for such high stakes. But then, 'tis said Mr. Glenister is very rich. Mrs. Sangster, whom I met at the lending library, declares he will set himself up as an English nabob, lording it over the neighbourhood like the princes in India.'

'Mrs. Sangster is a narrow-minded old busybody.'

'Hen! If *I* were to say that, you would be dreadfully shocked.'

'I dare say.' The governess' thin lips tightened. 'It is true, nevertheless. Had Mrs. Sangster a daughter of marriageable age she would speak differently. I declare I never saw such a stir amongst the mothers of Chichester since Mr. Langford lost his wife two years ago. It is quite degrading, the manner in which they are plying Mr. Glenister with invitations before he has been in the town a month.'

'I have heard he has declined them all.'

'Very sensible of him,' Miss Henty pronounced primly. 'In my opinion, a man should seek out a wife, not have a selection of candidates paraded under his nose like horses at a sale.'

'As I was before Lord Stansted,' Phyllida reminded her bitterly. She looked out of the window again. 'There is a great wagon approaching the house, and a horseman just leaving. Why, it is Kit!' She turned eagerly to the governess. 'Oh Hen, if he comes this way, pray allow me to speak to him.'

Miss Henty sighed. 'Very well. But we must not delay longer than a few minutes more.'

Joyfully Phyllida called for the carriage steps to be lowered. She waited for Kit by the roadside, her skirt and bonnet ribbons blown by the wind.

He reined in at sight of her, enveloping them both in a cloud of dust.

'It seems so long since I saw you,' she said as he dismounted.

'It is exactly three days,' he reminded her. 'We met by the Market Cross. Have you forgotten?'

'We did but pass the time of day, with the beast market taking place all around us.'

'Nevertheless, it could be termed seeing me.'

'Oh, you and your exactitude!' Her irritation passed in a moment, she was so delighted to be with him. 'You have been to "Lady Sarah's house"?'

'Yes. Mr. Glenister's daughter was taken ill. He sent for my father to go with all speed, but he was out, so I went.'

'Were you able to help?'

Kit drew himself up. 'Indeed, yes. It was but an attack of colic, due to the change of water, I think.'

Phyllida clasped her hands together. 'How clever you are, Kit. What is his daughter like?'

'A pretty child, though somewhat spoiled, I fear.'

She could not resist the temptation to question him about the house. 'It is, I suppose, very grand now?'

Kit answered enthusiastically. 'Indeed yes, but not vulgarly so, as some people in Chichester were prophesying. In fact . . .' He hesitated, then went on determinedly, 'In fact, the drawing-room is very like you pictured it, even to the harpsichord.'

'How can that be? I never spoke to him of . . .'

'I described it to him,' Kit revealed ingenuously. 'He asked me to tell him how you would have furnished it and I . . .'

'Kit, how could you? It is no affair of Mr. Glenister's in what manner I would have lived there.'

Kit reddened with embarrassment. 'He—he is very concerned at your disappointment, Phyllida. When I first went to him, at the inn . . .'

'Why did you do that? I have never had an opportunity to ask you.'

Kit scuffed the toe of his boot in the dusty road. 'Because you were so distressed. I do not rightly know what I hoped. Perhaps I had some wild notion that he might forfeit his claim.'

'That was *very* likely!' she exclaimed scornfully. 'A man of his type. Why, the gossip in Chichester is . . .'

'You should not listen to it. Mr. Glenister is, in fact, a most kind and generous man.' He hesitated, frowning down at the dusty track, then added awkwardly, 'I do not know whether I should tell you this. But he has offered to make it possible for me to go to a hospital in London to study medicine.'

She was astonished into silence. When she had recovered herself, she demanded, 'Why should he do that? Why concern himself in your affairs?'

'He questioned me about my future, then told me how he went out to India at fifteen and had to make his own way. He says if he can help a young man with ambitions and determination . . .'

'And you will accept this offer?'

'I should be foolish not to. My father is of the same mind, and most grateful to Mr. Glenister.'

'So! He not only steals my house but you, too.'

'Do not be absurd.' Kit's tone was impatient.

'Is he not providing the means to send you from me?' She turned away, near to tears.

Kit said desperately, 'Now that the manor house is no longer in Sir Francis's possession, you will most likely live in London when you are married. We could meet there.'

'You know I shall never be allowed to meet you. I shall be even less free then than now. And if, in what time is left to us, you are to go away . . .' She buried her face in her hands. 'I think I shall die if I cannot see you.'

'People do not die from disappointment,' he argued. 'Besides, if you really cared for me, you would be glad that I have this chance.'

'The chance to accept charity?' She saw by his face that she had gone too far.

He said grimly, 'Rest assured that I shall pay back every penny Mr. Glenister advances me. You are behaving childishly, Phyllida.'

'How do you expect me to behave? To clap my hands and dance a jig at the news that you are going away? Would that please you?'

He sighed, and chose his words more carefully. 'You know I do not want to be parted from you. But it is inevitable at some time. If only you would accept the situation.'

She said brokenly, 'My head accepts it. My heart will not.' She caught at his arm. 'Kit, I am so afraid.'

'Of what?'

'Of my marriage.'

'Oh, as to that, Mr. Glenister says . . .' he began cheerfully; then broke off, biting his lip.

She jerked up her chin, thrust out her lower lip. 'What, pray, has my marriage to do with Mr. Glenister? I' faith, I think he has bewitched you, you speak of him in tones of such veneration.'

He untethered his horse. 'One day *you* may speak of him more kindly,' he said earnestly. 'One day you may have much to thank him for.'

'Never!' she declared. 'He has taken "Lady Sarah's house" from me, and now he will take you. What is there to thank him for in that?'

The dust swirled up as he rode away, making her cough. She welcomed it. For when she met the footman's enquiring gaze, she was able to assert that the tears in her eyes were merely the result of grit thrown up by the hooves of Kit's brown cob.

The invitation came a week later. Mr. Glenister requested the pleasure of Miss Marchant's company, together with that of Miss Henty, for tea with him and his daughter the following Tuesday. He would consider it an honour for Miss Marchant to be his first visitor.

Phyllida's immediate reaction was to refuse. How could she bear to enter that house now it belonged to someone else? How be civil to its owner, who now planned to send Kit from her?

Miss Henty remarked, 'How very thoughtful of him, to invite you before anyone else.'

'Thoughtful! I vow he wishes to flaunt his possession of the place before my very nose.'

'You are being childish.'

'That is what Kit said. Very well, I *shall* be childish, and not go.'

She maintained that attitude for an hour, after which time curiosity proved too strong. She penned a note of acceptance, as short as possible within the bounds of politeness.

On Tuesday afternoon she tried Lucy's patience to the utmost by her several changes of mind about the gown she would wear. At last, arrayed in soft lilac wool and a green velvet bonnet with a large bow under the chin, she joined Miss Henty in the waiting carriage. She sat primly erect, determined that there should be no charge of childishness on this outing, that not even the critical eyes of her governess should find the slightest fault with her behaviour.

The gates of the manor were wide open and as they clattered up the drive she saw that many improvements had been made. The garden had been cleared of weeds; overgrown bushes clipped, branches lopped to let more light into the downstairs rooms. The brass handle on the front door gleamed against white paint, and as they drew up, the door opened smoothly on oiled hinges.

Phyllida bunched her skirt, bent her head to avoid knocking her bonnet and, accepting the footman's proffered hand, descended the steps. With all the dignity at her command, she advanced under the portico and into the hall. There, her composure abruptly deserted her. The servant, bowing low just inside the door, was dark skinned, dressed in the most exotic clothes she had ever seen. She was so taken aback that she stared openly. He wore a surcoat of kingfisher blue with a broad gold sash around his waist. His head was covered with a close fitting bulky white cap of the strangest shape, in the front of which gleamed a single jewel. When he straightened up, he seemed to tower above her and his thick black beard jutted forward.

His soft voice belied his fearsome appearance. 'If you please, memsahib, come this way.'

Swiftly she regained her composure and followed him. When he stood aside in the doorway of the drawing-room, she was again so startled she could not refrain from exclaiming aloud. It was as Kit had said. The room was just as she had pictured it so many times: the flowered carpet, crystal chandelier. In one corner was a cabinet full of china figures; in another, a harpsichord.

Now, in place of the hazy human figures who had peopled the room in her childhood fantasies, instead of Sir Francis Delaney stepping out of his portrait, there was Edward Glenister. As he came towards her, he seemed to make the room vibrate with colour. He wore white silk breeches and an embroidered waistcoat under a crimson topcoat. Against his tanned skin, his hair, bleached by the sun, appeared almost white. The effect was striking and, she had to admit, oddly attractive. Beside even the handsomest men of the neighbourhood he would stand out. He would make Kit, in his sombre shades of brown, look quite dull.

She heard Miss Henty clearing her throat pointedly,

and held out her hand. 'How very kind of you, sir, to invite us.'

He bent over her hand, raising it to his lips. 'It is you who are kind, ma'am, for accepting my invitation. You were observing my drawing-room. It is to your liking?'

'It is exactly as I would have furnished it myself,' she answered, but there was no approbation in her voice.

He smiled down at her. 'Perhaps I cheated a little. Having no wife to consult, and fearing that if I asked the advice of any lady in the town, it would set the gossips talking, I sought help from Mr. Burrell. It seems you had spoken often to him of your plans, he knew them by heart. So, without asking your permission, I put them into practice. Are you very angry with me?'

She sat stiffly on the most upright chair she could see, and folded her hands in her lap.

'You are naturally at liberty, sir, to furnish as you wish. Doubtless I should be flattered that you thought my plans worthy of adopting.'

He raised one eyebrow and glanced quizzically at Miss Henty who was seating herself comfortably in a silk covered armchair.

'I understood we were to have the pleasure of meeting your daughter,' she said.

'She will be down at any moment. The choice of a gown for this important occasion seemed to cause her some difficulty.'

A familiar gleam came into the governess' eyes. 'Am I to understand, Mr. Glenister, that you allow a child of six to choose what she wears?'

He paused with his hand on the bell rope. 'Is that so very bad for her? Perhaps I indulge her too much. She was left motherless at the age of four and a half and, like my late wife, she is not robust.'

'A cold water bath every morning would soon set her up.'

Edward jerked at the rope. 'I must disagree with you, ma'am. After the heat of India, it would most likely kill her.'

Colour showed in Miss Henty's cheeks. Phyllida bent her head to hide her amusement. She had endured much at the governess' hands: the iron collar and stiff board to keep her back straight, the heavy book on her head to teach her deportment; her knuckles rapped when she made blots or spelt words incorrectly. The servants too went in awe of Henty. It seemed she had at last met her match.

Their host gestured towards the harpsichord. 'While they are preparing tea, will you not favour us, Miss Marchant?'

Phyllida demurred, more to gain her governess' approval, than from disinclination. In fact, she welcomed the chance of action. It seemed to her unreal that she should be sitting here, in *her* house, in *her* drawing-room, as a visitor. The stiffness which had now arisen between herself and Edward Glenister seemed equally unreal after the easy manner of their first meeting.

She was in the middle of her second piece when she heard the door open quietly. Supposing it to be a servant bringing tea, she continued playing. The piece ended, she turned to acknowledge her host's applause.

A little girl stood within the circle of his arm, leaning against his knee. She was dressed in a simple blue gown, the soft folds accentuating the delicate structure of her body. Her ringlets were almost as fair as her father's hair, and her eyes had the same hazel colouring. In contrast to his, her skin was very pale.

He withdrew his arm from her waist. 'Go and greet Miss Marchant.'

The child obeyed him immediately. Her face earnest with concentration, she approached Phyllida and sank in a deep curtsey, betraying only the slightest wobble.

Phyllida held out her hand. 'So you are Emma? I have looked forward to meeting you. That is a very pretty gown you are wearing.'

The hazel eyes, wide and solemn, brightened. 'I am glad you like it, ma'am. I—I did not know which one to wear for this meeting.'

'Was it so important?'

'Oh yes. You are our first guest in our new home. Are you going to play again? May I stand beside you? I will not make a sound.'

Phyllida smiled down at her. 'Of course you may.'

She was very conscious of the child, standing absolutely still beside her, watching her fingers intently. When she came to the end of the piece she said, 'You appear very interested, Emma. Can you play?'

The little girl shook her head, gazing solemnly into Phyllida's face. 'Not yet, ma'am. But Papa says, if we can find a teacher . . .'

'I could teach you.' As soon as she had spoken, Phyllida realised her mistake. She could not imagine what had prompted so foolish an impulse. Apart from the impropriety of such a suggestion, she was totally unused to children.

Edward came to her rescue. 'That would be taking too great an advantage of your kindness, I fear, Miss Marchant. Perhaps you or Miss Henty could suggest a suitable person.'

The governess answered at once. 'Miss Eliza Stringer teaches most of the children in our neighbourhood and is a gentlewoman.'

'Thank you,' he said gravely. 'I will certainly approach her if you will be kind enough to give me her address. When we are more settled, there will also be the question of a governess.'

Phyllida saw again the gleam in Miss Henty's eyes. She knew full well that were the governess free, she would be only too willing to take on this task herself.

'I do not know of anyone suitable at the moment, sir,' Miss Henty said, 'but I will make some enquiries. Doubtless you would require someone of considerable education. You yourself . . .'

'I myself,' he broke in, 'was educated in the hardest school, experience. I did not go to university nor make the Grand Tour. I started work at fifteen as a writer in the East India Company in Madras, and studied in the little spare time I had.' He glanced up as the door opened. 'Ah, here is Dasim Ali with tea. Miss Marchant, have you any objection to Emma remaining?'

The child's eyes, full of appeal, were on her face. 'I shall be happy for her to do so,' she answered warmly. 'Come, Emma, you shall sit beside me and tell me about India.'

When Phyllida resumed her seat on the hard chair, the little girl sat on a stool at her feet, carefully arranging her skirts.

'What do you wish to know, ma'am?' she asked, adopting the formality of her father's manner.

'Anything you please, since I am totally ignorant on the subject.'

The child cast an appealing look at her father. Smiling, he explained. 'Miss Marchant means she does not know anything about India. She has never been there.'

'I as sorry,' Phyllida said, embarrassed. 'I did not realise you would not understand me.'

Emma said earnestly, 'I know a great many long words, both in English and Hindustani.'

'That is the language of India?'

'One of them. The Indians have many languages. Do they not, Dasim Ali?'

It was absurd, unreasonable. But her reaction was too swift for reason to play any part in it. The word 'Indian', the brown hand proffering cup and saucer . . . She was back in that nightmare of thirteen years ago. She drew back, knocked the servant's arm. The cup toppled, tea spilled in the saucer.

'I am sorry,' she blurted out, confused, the blood rushing hotly into her cheeks. 'That was clumsy of me.'

She saw the governess' disapproving frown, Edward Glenister's puzzled expression. It was Emma who came to her rescue.

'You have no need to be afraid of Dasim Ali,' she whispered. 'He only *looks* fierce.'

She spoke to the Indian servant in his own language and he smiled and bowed to Phyllida, then handed her another cup of tea. She felt ashamed before his complete imperturbability. Watching him move about the room with an air of impassive dignity, she could not imagine how even for a moment she could have connected him with those brown-skinned and befeathered savages who had murdered her parents.

Emma was saying, 'What I liked best in India were the snake charmers. I think you do not have snake charmers in England?'

'Indeed, we do not!' Miss Henty exclaimed in a shocked voice. 'What a barbarous form of entertainment.'

Their host said equably, 'They are merely using a form of hypnotism produced by music on a bamboo reed. Like Emma, I find it fascinating.'

For the second time Phyllida saw the governess discomfited, yet from his tone it was obvious he meant no offence. It occurred to her that here was a man who would state his views without fear or favour, whatever the company; a man who would brook little opposition to his will, though he might never raise his voice or make a violent gesture.

She asked the child, 'How do you travel in India? By carriage, as in England?'

'Only in the towns. In the country we go on river boats or by ox cart. The Indian princes travel on elephants, in a little house which sits on the elephant's back. Have you ever seen an elephant, ma'am?'

'No,' Phyllida answered regretfully. Out of the corner of her eye she saw the servant withdraw. The opening and closing of the door made no sound.

'I will draw you a picture of one, when we have finished tea,' Emma offered. 'They are very big animals. I was allowed to ride on one once, when Papa was in the army and he was visiting an important Indian prince in his palace.'

Puzzled, Phyllida turned to her host. 'I understood you were a merchant, Mr. Glenister.'

'In India, Miss Marchant, to use Mr. Shakespeare's words, "One man in his time plays many parts". An employee of the East India Company may start as a writer —which is to say, a clerk—and find himself become a soldier, even a politician, of necessity. The King's army was not sufficient always to defend the Company's possessions, so it created its own officers from volunteers. That was how Lord Clive pursued his career. First a civilian, then a soldier, a return to the civil service, and finally Commander-in-Chief, and Governor of Bengal. And what a blessing for England that was.'

'You admire Lord Clive?' she asked in surprise. 'I have heard my uncle say . . .'

His expression silenced her. He said grimly, 'With due respect to you, ma'am, your uncle was proved wrong. Lord Clive should never have been submitted to the humiliation of last year's trial, especially at the behest of such men as Lord Stansted and your guardian, men who . . .' He checked himself. 'I beg your pardon. The very thought of it fills me with such anger that I had best keep silent.'

'On the contrary, sir,' she said coldly, 'it would be better if you came into the open with your opinions. You have already made veiled insinuations against Captain Delaney to whom I am betrothed. You now do the same with my guardian, a gentleman who holds a most eminent position in the Company by which you were employed. Ah, I see.' She was aware of the child's anxious eyes moving from one to the other, but the antagonism this man aroused in her was again beyond control. 'It is *because* he holds that position, and because Captain Delaney holds a regular commission and is not a part-time officer, that you are moved by jealousy to . . .'

'Phyllida!' Miss Henty's voice sounded as shocked as she had ever heard it. 'You will apologise at once.'

Edward rose and stood with an arm along the mantelpiece. 'There is no need,' he said quietly. 'Miss Marchant is as entitled to her opinion as I am to mine. I have already remarked upon her loyalty, it does her great credit. I could only wish it were not so misplaced.' He turned to Phyllida. 'But I do assure you, ma'am, that I have only one reason to be jealous of Captain Delaney or Mr. Gunter—that they hold so high a place in your esteem.'

She was completely at a loss. When she argued with Kit, he argued back. When she grew angry with him, he either laughed at her or matched her anger with his own. But this calm indifference; this manner of turning aside her furious thrusts . . . It was as if she thought herself using a sword, to find it was only a frail reed. She felt humiliated, before Miss Henty and the child, and knew in her heart she had brought it upon herself. There was only one thing to do now. She half-rose, determined to leave. Then, startled, sank back into her chair.

Standing near the door was a woman whose entry had been as silent as the butler's, and of whom neither Edward Glenister nor his daughter had taken the slightest notice. Instead of a proper gown she was draped from shoulders to toes in pale blue cotton and a fold of the same material covered her head, revealing only a glimpse of black hair. There was a gold bangle on her brown arm, gold embroidery on her sandals. When momentarily she raised her extraordinarily dark eyes, they seemed to flash with the same brilliance. She was young and, even to English eyes, beautiful.

Miss Henty, following Phyllida's astonished gaze, rose stiffly and set her shoulders very square.

'I think,' she said icily, 'it is time we left.'

Phyllida was further startled to hear a chuckle from their host. When he spoke, his amusement was evident in his voice.

'You are mistaken, ma'am, in your assumption. This is Emma's ayah—her nurse.'

Relief showed in the governess' face, although she reddened with embarrassment. 'I beg your pardon, Mr. Glenister. We in Sussex are not used to—to the ways of the East.'

The amusement was still in his eyes as he bowed an acknowledgment of her apology. He spoke to the native woman in her own language and she moved silently forward.

Emma exclaimed, 'Must I go now, Papa? May I not be allowed to wave to Miss Marchant from the front door?'

'I think not. The air grows cool in the evening and you have had sufficient excitement for one day.'

For a moment rebellion showed in the child's face. Then she lowered her eyes and curtsied. 'Very well, Papa.'

The curtsey was repeated, as a mere bob, to Miss Henty. When she turned to Phyllida, she held out her hand.

'Goodbye, Miss Marchant. Will you come again soon? And will you bring your music and teach me how to play, as you said?'

'Emma,' her father said reprovingly. 'Go with ayah at

once. Miss Marchant made an impulsive offer which I am sure she now regrets. I think she will not even visit us again.'

The child looked from one to the other, the inability to comprehend their behaviour evident in her face. She bent her head, but Phyllida saw on her lashes the glitter of tears.

'I am sorry, ma'am,' she whispered. 'It—it would have been nice. Goodbye.'

Phyllida glanced helplessly at Miss Henty, but the governess' gaze was on the Indian woman, taking in every detail of her appearance. The servant stood quite still, eyes downcast. Edward Glenister still leaned negligently against the mantel-piece, straightening a log with his foot. She felt as if she were alone in the room, alone with the child who stood before her with bent head; waiting, she supposed, for a word from her. She saw the convulsive movement as Emma swallowed hard to control her tears, heard the suppressed sniff.

A surge of protectiveness, as fierce as anger, caught Phyllida unawares. She heard herself saying, as if the decision was inevitable, 'I did mean what I said, Emma. If your father will give his permission, I will teach you to play on the harpsichord.' She rushed on, before anyone could stop her. 'Perhaps he will allow your—your nurse to bring you to Meadhayes, in Chichester, where I live.'

Emma caught Phyllida's hand and held it against her wet cheek. She gazed up with brimming eyes which sparkled like summer raindrops. Phyllida bent and kissed her. She did not dare look at Edward Glenister.

She heard his voice, impersonal, holding no warmth. 'You are very kind, ma'am. On Emma's behalf, I accept your offer with the utmost gratitude.'

Emma bobbed a quick, ungraceful curtsey and ran to the door. As it closed silently behind the Indian nurse,

Phyllida could hear the little girl's voice, excitedly raised, chattering in the strange language of which she herself could not understand a word. It seemed to her then, and throughout the journey home, that her own behaviour was no less strange and startling than anything she had witnessed that afternoon. She had had the chance to put an end to her acquaintance with Edward Glenister; never in the future to have the slightest connection with the man who had robbed her of 'Lady Sarah's house', who was sending Kit away from her, and who so obviously was the enemy of both her future husband and her guardian. Her antagonism, she saw now, was well founded. Yet all in a moment she had allowed those feelings to be swept aside. She had been defeated, in the end, by a child's tears. What further hurt and humiliation that sudden weakness would cause her, she did not dare to consider.

V

Emma came to Meadhayes twice a week, in the new carriage drawn by four splendid greys. Impatiently she suffered the ayah to take off her coat and bonnet, then, skirts bunched, rushed into the drawing-room, executed the sketchy curtsey of which Miss Henty so disapproved, and scrambled on to the music stool. Perched on a cushion beside Phyllida, her short fingers tentatively prodding at the notes, she eagerly repeated their names, her face earnest with concentration.

She absorbed knowledge quickly, and it was not only music she wanted to learn. Over cups of chocolate when the lesson was ended, she would fire questions at Phyllida, scarcely waiting for an answer before she was off on another tack. What did people eat in England? Was it always so cold? Did nobody have native servants except her father? Why were there no pets in this house? In India she had had a little dog, and a bright bird in a cage.

'My uncle does not like animals in the house,' Phyllida told her.

'Your uncle? Where is he? I have never seen him,' Emma objected. 'Why do you live with an uncle? Where are your Mama and Papa?'

'They are both dead.'

'Like Mama. Did they die of cholera, too?'

Phyllida hedged. 'It was in America. I do not think they have cholera there.'

'Did you come from America in a ship, like we did from India?'

'Yes. I scarcely remember it. I was only five years old.'

Emma's eyes widened. 'But I am only six and I remember our journey quite well. It was not at all nice. We were shut up in a cabin and I was ill and so was Papa and ayah was not allowed to be in the same cabin and I scarcely saw Dasim Ali at all.'

'He is your native servant?'

'Yes. The one who frightened you. But he would not hurt you. He was servant to a parson before he came to Papa and it was then that he became a Christian. So now he loves everybody, especially Papa. Of course,' she reflected, head on one side, 'I can understand why he startled you. He does look fierce sometimes, as if he would like to kill somebody. But I do not suppose he ever will, not now.'

'Emma, you must not talk like that.'

'Why not? Indians like to kill people, each other and the English, and the English kill them too. The English killed lots of Indians at a place called Plassey. They were led by Lord Clive. Papa spoke to Lord Clive once. It was a long time ago, before he married Mama. Papa thinks Lord Clive is a wonderful man and it makes him sad to know that he is unwell now.'

'Lord Clive is unwell?'

'Yes. Papa says he is ill in his body from all his years in India and ill in his mind from what his enemies in England have done.'

Phyllida asked increduously, 'Emma, do you mean to say that your father talks of such matters to you?'

'Oh yes,' the child answered airily. 'He has no-one else to talk to, and neither have I. We have talked to each other since I was a very little girl. Mama would not listen to either of us, so we com—comforted each other.'

'Why would your mother not listen to you?' Phyllida asked, though she felt she should not have encouraged these disclosures.

'She was always ill and tired, and—and cross.' Emma's eyes were troubled. 'She was always cross with Papa and then he would look sad and go away, or he would take me for a ride or to see the snake charmer or the jugglers and sword swallower if they were in the town. The jugglers would make me laugh and then Papa would laugh too and that made me happy. Because he was sad such a lot of the time. He still looks sad, doesn't he, Miss Marchant?'

Taken aback, Phyllida answered hesitantly, 'I—I have seen so little of him, dear.'

That was true. He had brought Emma on the first occasion and Phyllida, against her own inclination but at Henty's prompting, had invited him in for a glass of wine. With the mixture of gravity and amusement she found so disconcerting, he had declined.

'Emma's presence here will be cause enough for comment,' he had told her. 'Mine, for any length of time, would set the gossips' tongues to wag in earnest, and I have no wish to embarrass you further.' Then he had smiled ruefully and added, 'Besides, I believe myself to be so greatly in disfavour with you that it is only the greatest generosity on your part which prompts you to do this kindness for my daughter.'

Emma said, breaking into her thoughts, 'I think you do not like Papa. Why is that, ma'am?'

'You must not ask such questions,' Phyllida answered, and was surprised to hear a distinct echo of Miss Henty in her own voice.

'I wish you did like him,' the child said regretfully. 'I think it makes him sad that you are not kind to him.'

'You are talking nonsense, Emma,' she said even more sharply. 'I am assured it does not matter to him one jot in what manner I treat your father. He has far more important matters to be concerned about.'

And so had she. The very next day Kit sent a note asking her to meet him at the derelict cottage on the downs, for he had some news to give her. By the greatest good fortune Henty had developed one of her headaches, so bad that she was past caring what her charge was doing. Phyllida bade Harry wait near the city wall, then rode on alone. Her route was along the same track where Centaur had bolted and thrown her, where Edward Glenister had rescued her. Just up there by the clump of hawthorns, their berries bright red now, she had fallen asleep after drinking his wine, and wakened to find him gazing at her with the utmost concern in his eyes. He had spoken so kindly then, and so gently wiped the dirt from her face, as if she were no older than Emma. Which was but one more reason to dislike him, she reminded herself angrily, since she was *not* a child and he had no right to treat her as one. 'Little Miss Phyllida' he had called her, by his tone reducing her to the same status as his daughter.

Kit was waiting by the broken wall of the cottage. As he lifted her down, she spoke her thoughts aloud, as she had always done with him. His face took on the stubborn look which meant he was about to argue with her.

'You are no judge,' he told her as he led her to a bank sheltered from the wind. 'You twist people's characters to fit your own wishes. I remember the romantic notions you used to have about Sir Henry Delaney and his wife, and now you expect their son, whom you are to marry, to be a paragon of all the virtues. You deem your uncle nothing but a worthy, upright man, yet Mr. Glenister . . .'

She rounded on him, the leather of her glove taut as she gripped her whip. 'Are you trying to tell me that Uncle Samuel is a rogue, that Sir Francis is a—a villain, and that Mr. Glenister is a perfect saint beside them?'

Kit opened his mouth to expostulate, but as so often in their association, the sight of her anger made him laugh.

'Phyllida, you are impossible! You have no logic, no sense of proportion.'

Flushing, she turned away, gouging out a stone with her heel. 'Then it is as well we cannot marry. For I declare I should not suit you.'

He took hold of her hand. 'Love does not take account of what is suitable.'

She faced him at once, her eyes pleading. 'Then you do love me, Kit?'

'Of course I do. I always shall. And . . .' It was his turn now to scuff at the loose stones. 'Phyllida, I want you to believe that—that when I go away, it will not make any difference. I shall be thinking of you, wanting to be with you.'

It was as if the wind had crept round the corner of the cottage and blown down her back.

'When you go away,' she repeated bleakly. 'You said in your note that you had something to tell me. What is it?'

He released her hand and leaned forward, his own clasped between his knees. 'I am leaving for London next week.'

'Oh.' She pressed her hands to her cheeks. 'So soon?'

'The sooner I go, the sooner shall I be trained. Mr. Glenister has arranged it all, through his sister, and . . .'

'I might have known. That man is intent on causing me unhappiness.'

Kit rounded on her. 'Phyllida, you are to stop maligning him. He has been most generous, he has our welfare at heart.'

'*Our* welfare! How can you say that? He may have yours, I allow you that. But how your absence can benefit me, I am at a loss to understand.'

He stared at the ground, frowning. 'It is impossible for me to explain. Indeed I do not myself fully comprehend what he has in mind. He asked me to trust him to see that all things would come right in the end. And I do.'

'And you dare to call *me* illogical, impossible!' she flared. 'Indeed, I declare you are bewitched by that man. Perhaps his black servant has put a spell upon you.'

Kit curbed his impatience. 'Phyllida, this is probably our last meeting for a long time. Are you going to spend it quarrelling?'

'No. Oh, no. It is just that . . .' She strove to control her voice. 'That I am so unhappy. You are right about my attitude towards Sir Francis. I *want* to believe that the man I am to marry is at least someone I may like and respect, since I may not have you. Yet it seems . . . Has Mr. Glenister spoken to you of Sir Francis?'

A cloud passed over the sun and she was not sure whether the change in Kit's expression was caused by that, or from within. He answered cautiously, 'He has mentioned him a time or two.'

'He does not like him, that he has made clear enough.'

'You are right. He does not like him.'

She tossed her head. 'Then that should be sufficient recommendation. Any man of Mr. Glenister's stamp . . .'

Seeing Kit's mouth tighten, she broke off. 'Oh Kit, perhaps I am jealous. I fear you hold him in greater regard than you do myself.'

He took her face between his hands. 'Phyllida, you are being foolish. Mr. Glenister is helping me to fulfil an ambition which otherwise seemed impossible. For that, I am grateful to him. It is perfectly natural, and affords no cause for jealously on your part.'

She had thought he was about to kiss her. To her disappointment he released her and adopted again his hunched-up, thinking attitude.

'Phyllida,' he said solemnly, 'I want you to give me a promise.'

'The promise I would have given you, were it possible, is to wait for ever for your return.'

He frowned and moved impatiently. 'Yes, I know. But the present is what concerns me now, and the immediate future. It may well be that you will need advice in a certain matter. Miss Henty may not be of much help to you, and I shall not be at hand.'

'Kit, you frighten me. In what matter?'

'I cannot explain. I want you to promise that, if you do need help, and there is no-one else to turn to, you will go to Mr. Glenister.'

She drew back. 'Are you mad? You ask me to go to *that* man?'

He raised his head and looked steadily at her. 'If it were possible, I would choose to leave you in his care while I am in London.'

'In *his* care!' she repeated incredulously. 'You would want me to live in the house he stole from me, with a savage who might murder me in my bed and a native woman creeping up behind my chair? You are suggesting I should sleep under the same roof as a cheat and a . . . a . . .'

Kit rose to his feet and she saw that this time she had

gone too far. He said coldly, 'One day you will be sorry for those words, for your whole attitude towards him. One day you *may* need his help. He may well be the only person who *can* help you.'

She rose unsteadily to face him. Above them a lark soared, singing as rapturously as if it were high summer. She heard a sheep cropping nearby, the high-pitched whistle of the breeze through a crack in the wall. Familiar sounds, as the cloud shadows moving across the downs were familiar; unchanging from one year to another. But for her this last hour had changed everything.

'Kit, please Kit, don't be angry with me,' she pleaded. 'I am distressed by your going away, and you frighten me. This matter in which you think I may need help— is it connected with my betrothal, my marriage to Captain Delaney?' She read the answer in his face without the need for words. She said jerkily, 'But—but surely, should I be faced with difficulties, unhappiness, in that respect, I have but to approach Uncle Samuel . . .' She broke off at the negation in his eyes. 'Kit, tell me . . .'

'Yes, I will tell you,' he said harshly. 'It is time you knew something of the truth. Your Uncle Samuel bought his place on the Court of Directors of the East India Company by arranging your betrothal to Lord Stansted's heir.'

She stared at him, doubting she had heard aright. 'How can you say such a dreadful thing?'

'Because it is true,' he answered bluntly.

'Who told you? Oh, you have no need to answer. Mr. Glenister . . .'

'He did but confirm what I have long suspected. Miss Henty knows it too, I am certain.'

'I do not believe it. I *will* not.'

'There you go again, ignoring the truth whenever it suits you, believing only what you choose.'

'If I believe this, it means that—that Uncle Samuel

cares nothing for my feelings.'

'Had you reason to suppose he did?'

His tone roused her to a desperate affirmation. 'He has been most generous, he has never stinted me of . . .'

'Clothes? Jewels? Naturally he would not begrudge you such things. Brought up as a young woman of society, even as narrow a society as exists in Chichester, you are a more saleable produce.'

'*Kit!*' She buried her face in her hands. 'That was the cruelist thing I ever had said to me in all my life.'

'I am sorry,' he apologised quickly. 'Truly, Phyllida, I am sorry. It is anger, frustration, that made me speak so. Do you not see that I am as unhappy as you about this marriage? But I can do nothing to help you. Come, look at me.'

Gently he pulled her hands from her face. 'There is only one thing I *can* do, and that is to tell you where help may be found should you need it.'

'With Mr. Glenister?' she asked bitterly.

'Yes.'

'You are asking me to accept him in your place?'

'No, not that. I only ask you to trust him. The need may not arise. If it does, go to him.'

She looked at Kit, memorising every detail of his face against the parting which was to come.

'Very well,' she said at last. But in her heart she knew she would not do as he urged. Nor would she even admit that there could possibly be any situation in which she would be driven to seek help from a comparative stranger.

Kit kissed her then, holding her as if she were a fragile piece of china. She leaned her head against his shoulder.

'Oh, Kit, if only we could be married.'

He said almost roughly, 'You have no idea what marriage means.'

'You could teach me. You could teach me everything, couldn't you, Kit?'

He put her from him and said abruptly, 'We must go back. It grows cold up here and my father will have need of me. I would that someone in my absence would tell you what marriage . . . Oh, but what is the use?'

On the track leading to the city, he reached across and took her hand. 'You will write to me, Phyllida? I will send word when I have found permanent lodgings.'

'Of course, every week. And you?'

'I shall be kept very busy, I surmise, but I will write as often as I can.' His face brightened. 'I can scarce believe it is really happening, that soon I shall be in London, working at the hospital.'

She saw that his thoughts had turned away from her already. She had played but a small part in his life. In the future she would play none at all. Again she felt as if the wind were blowing down her back. When he rode away from her as they came within sight of the city walls, she actually shivered despite her warm riding habit. But not until she was alone in her own room did she give way completely to her grief.

Kit had gone. Miss Henty had suffered a series of violent headaches and lay exhausted in her darkened bedroom. There was no-one to talk to, no-one to confide in. Bored and dispirited, Phyllida went about her household tasks. She completed a piece of tapestry she had been working on for months, painted a little, read a little. She attended a dull tea-party, paid a visit to the mercer's and the lending library. With growing apprehension she awaited the arrival of each mail. The roads were becoming very bad now and the coach was often delayed by a broken wheel or shaft, or a horse foundering. To her surprise and delight she received a short letter from Kit, giving her an address to which to write. To her relief there was none from her uncle to give her news of the return of her betrothed from India. She felt herself to be living in a kind of vacuum, longing for something to break the monotony, yet dreading any change.

It was therefore with increased pleasure that she looked forward to the afternoons when Emma came for her music lessons. The sight of the little girl's face, cheeks flushed, eyes bright, brought a lifting of her own spirits. She gave the child some measure of joy, and Emma gave it back to her. For the first time in her life she experienced a relationship which caused her no anxiety. There was no striving to win Emma's devotion, no constant seeking for reassurance of affection as with Kit or Henty. Emma's affection was hers for the taking. And she gave of her own freely to the child, without self interest and was made happy in the giving.

There came a day when Edward Glenister's carriage fell victim to the appalling condition of the Winchester road and he himself brought Emma into Chichester, riding pillion on his bay mare. Again he declined Phyllida's stiff invitation to step inside, and rode off, promising to collect his daughter in two hours' time.

That same afternoon Emma played three times running quite perfectly the little piece Phyllida had been teaching her.

'May I play it to Papa when he comes back?' she asked eagerly. 'Oh, please, ma'am, will you ask Papa to come in and hear me play?'

'We will see,' Phyllida answered non-committally.

She was sure he would not do so, especially as Henty was not present. Aware of her dislike and, she had to admit, mindful of her reputation, he would produce some polite excuse. His manner would be formal and courteous, making it impossible for her to say the angry words which seethed in her mind. She longed to rail at him, to give vent to the hurt and humiliation he had

caused her. But against his impassivity, his obvious indifference to her opinions despite the polite phrases, she
felt helpless.

This afternoon, she noticed, he had looked tired and
drawn; even pale beneath the tan and there had been a
heaviness about his eyes, as if he were not well. She
was disconcerted to discover how much she *had* noticed.
She was even more startled when, turning over a page
of music for Emma, she saw, not bars and notes, but
Edward Glenister's face in every detail. There were dark
flecks in his hazel eyes and fine lines at their corners.
There was a thin margin of white skin between his sun-
tanned forehead and fair hair, and if he moved his head
sideways, the lighter skin showed also below his cravat.
The backs of his hands had a light covering of fair hairs.
There was a tightness about the corners of his mouth
as if, even when he smiled, he was holding himself in
check.

She shook her head, as if that would clear her vision,
and chided Emma sharply for a wrong note. The child
looked up at her in astonishment.

'You sound just like Mama.'

'Do not be foolish,' Phyllida said in the same irritable
tone. 'You cannot possibly remember what your mother
sounded like.'

'Yes, I can. It was like this.' Emma spoke in a high,
whining voice. ' "Emma, don't do that, it is bad for my
head. Emma, be quiet. Edward, stop walking about the
room." And she looked like this.' The little girl put a
finger at each corner of her mouth and pulled them
down.

'Emma, you must not . . .'

'Why must I not? It is true, all I have said about
Mama.'

'You must keep to the truth, Phyllida. You twist people's characters to fit your own wishes.' Kit's voice now,

Kit's face replacing that other. That was better. It had been quite disturbing, as if Edward Glenister were actually in the room.

Phyllida said firmly, 'Nevertheless, she was your mother, and you should love her.'

'How could I, when she didn't love me? Papa loves me and I love him, and if you were my Mama I would not have to be told to love you. Because I do.'

'Oh, darling.' Phyllida held the child close. 'I am not old enough to be your mother.'

'Do you have to be very old to be somebody's mother?'

'No, not *very* old. I am . . .' I am quite old enough to be one, though not yours, she was about to say. She recalled how she had wandered about the rooms at 'Lady Sarah's house' imagining children at her skirts. It had all been part of the fantasy. Now, with this child pressed close to her side, the thought of bearing her own children gave her both pleasure and pain. She was again disturbingly aware of her own body, of the inexplicable ache and yearning deep inside her. But to have children you must have a husband. From the thought of that, since it involved the unknown, she shied away.

Edward Glenister was late in fetching his daughter. When he did come, Phyllida saw through the window how heavily he dismounted, that he swayed and passed a hand across his forehead; that his hands shook as he tethered the mare. For one dreadful moment she thought he might be drunk. Then she saw his face. Despite the tan, it had a pallor which alarmed her, with a patch of bright red on each cheek.

Impulsively, she went herself to open the front door. 'Mr. Glenister, what is the matter?'

He clutched at the door jamb for support. 'I am sorry,' he muttered. 'Is Emma ready? I must return home at once.'

'You are ill?'

'It is a—a fever. Do not be alarmed, I am quite used to it, and . . .' His words were cut off by the chattering of his teeth.

'You had best come inside,' Phyllida said.

'No, I—I . . .' A spasm of shivering stopped him, and again she heard his teeth chatter.

She said firmly, 'You will come inside, Mr. Glenister. You are certainly in no fit state to take Emma home at present.'

He looked at her as if he did not understand her words, and the shivering seized him again. She took him by the arm and half pulled him into the drawing-room where he sank heavily into a chair. Emma ran forward.

'Papa, what is the matter? Is it the fever?'

'Yes, I am afraid so.' He managed a wan smile and patted her hand. 'Do not look so anxious, I shall be all right in a moment.'

'You will not, Papa, you know you will not. You must go straight to bed with a hot brick at your feet and a bottle of claret.'

Phyllida tugged at the bell rope so urgently that the footman came running. 'Fetch rugs and blankets, some linen and a bowl of cold water,' she ordered. 'Then stay with Mr. Glenister while I make a hot posset. And, William, tell Silas to have the carriage ready as soon as possible. He must drive Mr. Glenister and his daughter home.'

Edward put out a remonstrative hand. 'I cannot possibly trouble . . .'

'You are in no state to argue, sir. I have learned from Kit how to deal with fevers. Come, Emma, you may help me make the posset.'

Emma looked solemnly up at her. 'He always has claret, ma'am. It is the only thing that makes him better.'

Phyllida hesitated, looking from daughter to father. Again he made an effort to smile. 'She is quite right. But

I would not dream of questioning your treatment. I am, for the moment, I fear, entirely in your hands.'

The dreadful shivering attacked him again. He thrust a finger between his chattering teeth. But he could not prevent the violent shaking of his whole body or keep his riding boots from knocking together. His eyes were unnaturally bright in his flushed face. She heard a little groan escape him as he dropped his head into his hands. He was in her hands, as he had said; at her mercy. And there was nothing in her heart but pity.

Emma clutched at her skirt. 'Will you not give him claret, ma'am, *please?*'

The footman came running down the stairs and across the hall, bearing an armful of blankets.

'William, do you know where to find some claret?' Phyllida asked.

'Yes, Miss Phyllida, of course.'

'Then bring a bottle at once, and a glass. Leave the blankets, I will deal with them.'

The servant's mouth opened, his eyes bulged. But he did as she bid him.

With Emma's help, she draped Edward in a cocoon of blankets. He clutched them to him, and the shivering was almost continuous and totally beyond his control. When William brought the bottle and uncorked it, swiftly Phyllida poured a glassful and offered it to Edward. Then, seeing that he was quite unable to manage the glass himself, she put it to his lips and steadied his head for him to drink. He gulped down the wine, and she poured another glass and he drank that down while Emma gazed anxiously on.

Phyllida, with one part of her mind, was aware of the sound of the carriage being trundled into the yard, the horses' hooves on the cobbles. She was relieved that Silas had caught the urgency of her instructions.

'Another glass?' she asked.

He shook his head. 'I—I am sorry to inflict this on you.'

'There is no need to apologise, Mr. Glenister. No-one can help being taken ill. They will soon bring the carriage round, and then William will assist you into it. Meanwhile, perhaps it will help to have a cold compress on your forehead.'

There seemed to be some complication in the stable yard. There was a deal of shouting and banging of doors, and it sounded as if the horses were giving trouble from the amount of shrill whinnying she could hear.

Emma stood close beside her as she dipped the linen in the bowl of water and wrung it out.

'It gets worse than this,' she whispered. 'Afterwards he is always very weak. Poor Papa. But that will help him,' she added as Phyllida applied the compress. 'It is what Dasim Ali does.'

Edward started as the cold linen was laid against his burning forehead. Then he looked up at Phyllida. In his eyes was so patent an expression of helpless gratitude that she felt her heart swell, then contract. He seemed to her then no older than Emma. She felt a disconcerting urge to put her arm around his shoulders and comfort him as she would have done his child. She gripped the back of the chair to prevent herself carrying out so foolish a notion. As if her impulse had imparted itself to him, his head fell forward against her breast and he clutched at her arm as the rigor laid hold of him again. His need was like a great wave breaking over her, washing away all the anger and hatred she had ever felt against him. She put her arm around his shoulders and held the cold compress against his head. The pain was deep inside her again, yet now it was mixed with a strange new happiness.

The side door opening, the heavy footsteps crossing the hall, seemed sounds from a long way off, so unreal that one voice sounded exactly like Uncle Samuel's. She felt surprisingly sorry that the servants had been so quick.

'William,' she began as she half turned towards the door.

Her gasp mingled with a whimper from Emma, the chattering of Edward's teeth. The hall was suddenly full of servants distractedly smoothing aprons, straightening wigs. In the doorway of the drawing-room, legs planted firmly apart, stomach thrust out, his brows drawn together in the fiercest of glares, was Uncle Samuel.

Just behind him stood a young man in a blue silk suit which matched his eyes, and a caped travelling coat. Phyllida saw the glint of gold on his sword hilt and the buckles of his shoes; noticed how tanned his skin was against the powdered wig. She was quite sure she had never seen him before. Yet there was something familiar about him.

'Who the devil is this fellow?' her guardian demanded.

'He—he is . . .' she began, her eyes still on the stranger.

Edward struggled to his feet, the blankets falling around him. He gripped the chair arm for support.

'My name is Glenister, sir. I apologise . . .' Then he, too, saw the young man. '*Delaney!*'

Phyllida caught her breath, put a hand to her throat in dismay. The young man stepped forward, took off his gold laced tricorne and made Edward a mocking bow.

'Your servant, sir. Though I will not say we are well met. In fact . . .' He surveyed Edward with eyes as mocking as his bow. 'Very ill met.' He laughed shortly at his own joke, then his glance went from Edward to Phyllida. 'From everyone's point of view, this seems to be an unfortunate moment. For this lady, I assume, is the one I have come home to marry.' The blue eyes surveyed her person in the same manner as his uncle's had done three years ago. She felt herself grow as hot as if she too had a fever.

When he spoke again, the scorn in Francis Delaney's voice was like the cut of a whip.

'And I was assured she was as innocent as the day she was born. It seems, Mr. Gunter, that you should have locked up your niece until they let me home from India.'

VI

Once again Phyllida wrenched at the handle of her bedroom door, knowing it was useless. For three hours, marked by the chimes of the clock on the Market Cross, she had been shut up here, just as if she were no older than Emma. And why? What had she done to deserve such punishment? It was bad enough to have been so peremptorily ordered to her room in front of the servants. But to be forced to walk across the hall and up the stairs in the silence which had followed her guardian's furious outburst, under the eyes of Edward Glenister, of Emma and, worst of all, of the man she was to marry, had been the most humiliating experience of her life.

She shut her eyes, trying to blot out that scene. But it was there before her closed lids. Clearly she saw the hard mockery in Francis Delaney's eyes, heard the whiplash of his voice, shocking her into silence so that she could not even attempt an explanation. It had been left to Edward to do that, and he had failed. Striving to control the chattering of his teeth, he had got as far as, 'Sir, you have no cause to upbraid Miss Marchant . . .' when Uncle Samuel had bellowed for William to throw him from the house.

From her bedroom window she had seen him stumble down the path, mount his horse and lift Emma up behind him with the greatest difficulty. Hunched in his riding coat, one hand gripping the pommel for support, he had ridden slowly up the street until the houses hid him from her view.

She could still hear Emma's whimper, see her frightened face. She could picture Henty, stumbling down the stairs, her dress crumpled, her cap awry, brown curls bobbing incongruously on her forehead.

With an impatient exclamation, Phyllida opened her eyes and continued her pacing of the room. Halting before her dressing chest, she picked up the portrait which had stood there for the past three years. In that young man downstairs, where was there any likeness to the youth who looked out at her from the painting? At seventeen his chestnut hair had curled against his pale cheeks. Now he wore a wig and his skin was burned by the Indian sun. His eyes were still blue, it was true, but instead of the youthful amusement she had found so attractive, she had seen nothing but scorn.

She flung the portrait across the room so that it fell face downwards on her bed.

For how much longer was she to be shut up here as if she had committed some dreadful crime instead of merely offering succour to a sick man? How was she to know her guardian was coming to Chichester? Or that her future husband was even in England since he had not troubled to acquaint her of the fact?

People passed along the street below her window. A carriage rolled over the cobbles. A hunchback beggar was making a methodical search of the central gutter, turning over refuse, scrabbling in the filth with bony fingers. Automatically, she fetched her reticule and, opening the window, flung him a coin. He grabbed at it and babbled his thanks. It was the second time she had earned gratitude that afternoon. Against her will, she recalled the expression in Edward Glenister's eyes which had so moved her. She had felt as protective towards him as towards Emma. Protective, towards the man who had caused her so much hurt, so much unhappiness, who had the ability to make her feel no older than his daughter? She did not understand. She only knew that this day had turned her world upside down.

At length she heard light steps in the passage. The key turned in the lock. Lucy's anxious face appeared around the door.

The maid said in a loud whisper, 'You're to come down now, ma'am. The master wishes to see you. In the little parlour.'

'Is anyone with him?' Phyllida was annoyed to hear how nervous she sounded.

'No, ma'am. The other two gentlemen have left. I've heard that Captain Delaney has taken himself off to the Dolphin and Anchor where he's putting up. 'Twas a great surprise, wasn't it, ma'am, him coming with the master like that, and none of us even knowing as Mr. Gunter was on his way? He told William as he'd written a week ago, but you know how the mail has been of late.'

Phyllida peered into the mirror as she smoothed her hair and adjusted the lace fichu at her neck. 'Where is Miss Henty?'

'In her room, Miss Phyllida. The master said she was to stay there. She's been weeping, I think. 'Tis my belief he might have dismissed her.'

Phyllida straightened abruptly. 'Dismissed Henty? But why? She was not even present when . . . Oh, that makes it worse, of course. Is my uncle still very angry?'

'He's in a proper pet, for sure. To my way o' thinking, he's no cause to be. Mr. Glenister's never behaved other than a proper gentleman and there wasn't a mite of harm in your having the little maid here. He couldn't help being took sick now, could he? A nasty mind the master has, I reckon—not that he's ever chased me down the passages like some as I've known. I'll say that for him.' She clapped a hand over her mouth. 'There now, whatever am I saying? You'd best come quickly, ma'am, afore we both get into more trouble.'

Phyllida did not go quickly. She walked leisurely along the passage, across the landing and down the stairs, shoulders squared, head held high. She had nothing whatever to be ashamed of, and she would face Uncle Samuel in that knowledge. There was nothing in the least to fear, she assured herself. Even if he *had* dismissed poor Hen, he could scarcely turn his own niece out of his house without a proper cause. And if Sir Francis had not liked what he saw of his future bride, then perhaps he would end the betrothal and she would be free. And if she were free, at least she could hope for the impossible, that one day she and Kit . . .

Uncle Samuel stood in his habitual attitude before the fire, legs apart, stomach thrust forward, hands beneath his coat tails. The heavy folds of his chin sagged on his linen cravat.

Phyllida entered the room with as much assurance as she could muster and curtsied low. He gestured towards a chair.

'Now, perhaps, miss, you are prepared to explain your conduct.'

'I tried to do so, sir, but you would not listen. I do assure you, there was nothing in the least improper in my conduct.'

'Are you out of your mind, girl?' His eyes bulged, his face took on a dull red tinge. 'I arrive home in the expectation of giving you the great pleasure of presenting your future husband to you. In the yard I find my carriage being got ready to transport home a stranger who has a perfectly good horse of his own at the gate. I enter the house and find you, with not a servant in sight and your governess conveniently in her bedroom, with your arms about this man and he in the act of making love to you. And in front of a child, to boot!' He raised his

hand as she sought to interrupt him. 'This disgraceful
exhibition is also witnessed by your betrothed. To cap it
all, the man in question turns out to be not only an
enemy of mine but also of Sir Francis Delaney's.'

'How can that be?' she asked dazedly.

'Mr. Glenister is an admirer of Lord Clive and doubtless made his fortune in the same reprehensible way, by
accepting bribes and presents, money which should have
gone by rights to the East India Company.'

'But was not Lord Clive completely exonerated from
that charge?'

Scornfully her guardian answered. 'Oh, certainly.
Those who had much to gain from his acquittal won the
day against us, harping on his past achievements, our
debt to him.'

Phyllida realised suddenly that if this subject could be
kept going, at least it would steer the conversation away
from herself. She said tentatively, 'Naturally I know little
of such matters, sir, but I understood that Lord Clive did
save India for us.'

'That gave him no excuse for reaping a private fortune
out of his victories. Nor men like Glenister for supporting him, and doubtless doing likewise. It is young men
like Captain Delaney we have to thank for protecting
our rights, preserving our honour, in India; men who
have no thought of personal gain, who seek only to serve
their country. To think that he should have seen you in
so compromising a situation.' He jerked his clenched
hands and his coat tails were almost singed by the flames
from the great logs in the fireplace. 'And there is another
thing. Your governess informs me that you have been
giving lessons to that chit of Glenister's. Since when have
you set yourself up as a common music teacher?'

'I offered to teach her out of—of charity, sir. The child
has no mother, no governess or nurse other than an Indian servant.'

'An Indian servant? You mean, a native woman?'

'Yes, sir.'

'So the rumours I heard are correct. Are there any other black servants there?'

'Yes, the butler. He is a Mohammedan, turned Christian.'

'Do they both wear native dress?'

'Yes, Uncle Samuel.'

'So. He sets himself up as a nabob of the first order, and on Company's money, while heroes like Delaney . . . Phyllida, do you realise the enormity of your conduct? Has it not been enough that you have had a disgraceful association with a mere physician's son? Have you *no* shame?'

She rose and faced him, hands clenched, her lower lip thrust out. 'Uncle Samuel, I do protest at your harsh judgment of me. I swear I have done nothing of which I am ashamed . . .'

'Enough of that kind of talk,' he declared. 'I want no show of your father's rebellious ways in this house. You seem to forget, miss, what you owe me. Where, I ask you, would you be now but for my interest in you? And what thanks have you rendered for all I have done for you? It is high time you were married, with a husband to put a stop to your wilful ways, and a covey of children at your skirts to keep you occupied. It is only to be hoped that by your own folly you have not ruined your chances; that Sir Francis will prove generous enough to overlook this afternoon's extraordinary exhibition.'

'And if he does not,' she began recklessly, then stopped abruptly as she recollected Kit's words: 'Your Uncle bought his place on the Court of Directors of the East India Company by arranging your betrothal to Lord Stansted's heir.'

She knew the real cause of her guardian's displeasure.

If Sir Francis should withdraw from the contract, what then would be Uncle Samuel's position? She knew herself utterly defeated. She was but a pawn in a game of power seeking and avarice. There was only one course open to her, as there had always been only one. That course was to submit.

She sat down, bent her head and folded her hands in her lap.

'If I have done wrong, I ask your pardon, sir. I will endeavour to act in future so that you may not find further fault in me. Neither you, for Sir Francis who I hope will find it in his heart to overlook my—my folly.'

She lay awake for a long time that night. The future appeared as dark as the space within the bed curtains. No Kit. The probability of no Henty. No 'Lady Sarah's house'. No Emma. Instead, London, the probability of meeting again the hated Lord Stansted; a strange house and servants, a new life of which she knew nothing, with a husband who already despised her. And her eyes opened regarding Uncle Samuel's true attitude towards her.

There was no way out. Toss and turn, thump the pillows as often as she may, she was powerless to alter anything. In the early hours of the morning she had the wild idea of running away. But where could she go? There was no one who cared a jot for her save Kit. He could not help her, he had said so often enough. Of course, there was Edward Glenister, according to Kit. She could just see herself knocking on his door, saying, 'I do not want to marry the husband chosen for me by my guardian. What can you do about it?'

And he would smile at her in that superior way and say airily, 'What did I tell you? And what would you have me do? I am not a magician, little Miss Phyllida.'

Then she remembered that he would be abed with fever, and even that fantastic picture faded. Again she heard the heavy tramp of the night watchman.

'Three o'clock and all's well.'

But all was not well with her. It was very far from well.

When she woke, very late next morning, the house seemed abnormally quiet. Lucy came quickly in answer to her bell.

'Gracious, ma'am, I began to think you were took bad as well.'

Phyllida sat up, stretching. 'Why should I be took . . . why should I be indisposed?'

'Everyone else seems to be. The master is abed with the gout and Miss Henty moaning in her room with the shutters tight closed and scarce able to lift her head from the pillow, poor soul.'

'I suppose that is due to yesterday's upset. *Has* Uncle Samuel dismissed her?'

'No, ma'am, seemingly not. I think she's to be allowed to stay until you're wed.'

The word made Phyllida pause with her legs dangling over the side of the bed. She said dully, 'When I am married, I suppose everything will be changed. They will not take *you* from me, surely?'

'I've heard nothing about that, Miss Phyllida. 'Tis to be hoped not, for how you'd have the least idea of time without Miss Henty or me I don't know. You'd best hasten now if you're not to keep Sir Francis waiting an unconscionable time.'

'Sir Francis is coming here?'

'In an hour, ma'am.'

'But how can I receive him, without either my uncle or Miss Henty present?'

The maid sniffed. 'What's wicked with Mr. Glenister is seemingly proper with the other gentleman. 'Tis queer to my way o' thinking. But then, I'm not gentry.'

Phyllida sat on the edge of the bed, staring at her bare feet, wriggling her toes. She asked slowly, 'Lucy, did you —did you form any opinion of Captain Delaney?'

The maid shook out the flounces of Phyllida's dressing wrapper. 'Maybe yes, maybe no. 'Tis best I keep silent.'

Phyllida looked up quickly. 'Then you did not like him?'

Lucy pursed her lips. ' 'Tisn't exactly a question of liking, ma'am. After all, it's not for such as me to do aught but what I'm told and keep my thoughts to myself. There's folks as treat you right and folks as don't.'

'And Captain Delaney is one that doesn't?'

The maid held out the wrapper. 'Come along now, miss, if you please.'

Slipping her arms into the garment, Phyllida asked, on an impulse, 'And Mr. Glenister, which is he?'

The maid's tone changed. 'Oh well, now, there's a proper gentleman. I'd trust *him* in the darkest of corners.'

'Lucy, what do you mean? Yesterday you spoke of Uncle Samuel not chasing you down dark passages, and now—this. Sir Francis remarked most scornfully that he understood I was as innocent as the day I was born. Kit says I do not know what marriage really means. How can I help being innocent if no one will tell me? Lucy . . .'

'No, miss, I'm sorry. I've had strict instructions from Miss Henty, and so's everyone else in the house. It's not right to my way o' thinking. But there, as I said, 'tisn't for the likes o' me to pass judgment. But I'd be a bit careful like, if I were you. Just make sure Captain Delaney keeps his hands to himself. Now I'm ready to brush your hair.'

Phyllida, suddenly realising what the maid had been doing, asked, 'Why have you put out my riding suit?'

'Because you are to ride with Sir Francis.'

'*Alone?*'

'Yes, ma'am, that's why I said to be careful. Oh,

Harry'll go with you, never fear, and I'll tell him he's to keep you in sight.' She began to brush Phyllida's hair with short jerky strokes. 'Sir Francis sent a note asking the master's permission, and your uncle was much in favour of the idea, seemingly. "Tell Miss Phyllida," he says, "it will be an excellent opportunity for them to get better acquainted." ' The maid sniffed again, loudly. 'I should say that's very likely, too.'

As Phyllida went down to breakfast her legs felt as if they did not belong to her, and her hands trembled so that knife and fork clattered against her plate. She looked out of the window, hoping to see rain clouds, but the sky was clear, the sun shining. Far from not being ready in time, it was she who did the waiting, for half an hour. A dozen times she glanced in the mirror, smoothed her skirt, adjusted a fold of her lace cravat.

Francis Delaney came at last, smiling, debonair, as bright as the morning in a saffron riding suit with a yellow waistcoat, the sun glinting on spurs and sword. He bowed low over her hand and smiled into her eyes and paid her extravagant compliments.

Her spirits rose like a rocket. She had expected to be further humiliated and censured by this man who had every right to take her to task. Instead, his manner was as easy as Kit's, and she saw him this morning as an older version of the youth in the portrait. She wondered if she could possibly have imagined that mocking look in his eyes, the scorn in his voice. He made not the slightest reference to the incident. Yesterday might never have been.

She was so relieved and delighted that she smiled back at him and laughed at his pleasantries. When he brushed Harry aside and aided her to mount Centaur, she made no protest. She even found the pressure of his fingers pleasant and when, seemingly without intention, his hand touched her ankle, she felt an odd little shiver of excitement run through her. She told herself there was nothing in the least to be afraid of. He was being kind and generous. For, after all, she reflected, it must have been a shock to have seen his betrothed, for the first time, with her arm around another man, however innocent that action had been on her part.

She said impulsively, 'Sir Francis, I am sorry—about yesterday. I trust you . . .'

He smiled up at her. 'There is no need to say any more, ma'am. I assure you, I understand—perfectly.'

She felt the colour flood into her cheeks. 'Thank you, that is most generous,' she murmured, and urged Centaur forward.

He mounted swiftly and caught up with her. 'But I think you owe me something, and so I shall ask you to grant me a favour. Oh, do not look so alarmed, it is a very small matter. I have a wish to see the house built for my mother. I believe it is a comfortable morning's ride.'

She looked at him in amazement. 'You surely do not mean to call upon Mr. Glenister?'

He threw back his head and laughed aloud. 'No, I do not intend any such thing, my dear. Did you suppose I meant to call him out in your presence?'

'To call him out,' she repeated in dismay. 'You—you would fight a duel with him?'

He glanced keenly at her. 'So the thought disturbs you?'

She said, avoiding his eyes, 'I did not suppose you had any cause to fight Mr. Glenister. Unless, of course, the matter of the house . . .'

'The house?'

' "Lady Sarah's house". Did he not win it from you gambling, after persuading you into playing with higher stakes than was—sensible?'

He made no reply and when she glanced at him his

face was thoughtful. After a moment he turned to her, smiling.

'That quarrel is over,' he answered easily. 'I do not bear malice for past wrongs. But you, my poor Phyllida . . . Were you very disappointed? You had, I believe, set your heart upon living in that house?'

She bit her lip. 'I was disappointed, it is true. I have grown used to the idea now.'

'Not so used that you would not like to live there, one day?'

'But it is not possible,' she said, puzzled.

'Everything is possible,' he remarked confidently. 'With money, one can gain most things one desires in life.'

'But how? Mr. Glenister . . .'

'Is a merchant, trained always to seek a profit. I have but to offer him a worthwhile sum . . .'

'You have such a sum?' she asked incredulously.

He leaned towards her and put a hand over hers. 'I shall have, when we are married. And to what better purpose could I put part of your dowry than to give you your heart's desire?'

She was completely taken aback. 'Oh, how wonderful that would be!'

He pressed her fingers and asked softly, 'Now are you willing to lead me there, at least to a vantage point where I may see it for myself?'

'Of course. With pleasure.'

It was beyond all her hopes. Last night everything had seemed lost to her: Kit, Henty, 'Lady Sarah's house', her trust in Uncle Samuel, all chance of happiness. This morning Henty was still with her, it seemed possible that she might after all have the house of her dreams, and this man, who had grown almost to an ogre in her imagination, was revealed as charming, thoughtful, and in no way to be feared. In time, perhaps, they might even come to understand each other quite well. Kit was lost to her. She had always known that must be so. As for Uncle Samuel, he must know what was best for her.

Kit's voice was like a barb under her skin. 'You twist people's characters to suit yourself. You believe what you want to believe.'

Was it not better that way? Of what use to try to probe beyond? It was best to accept people at face value, to accept the moment's happiness and put aside anxiety about the future.

She pointed out landmarks to Francis as they rode side by side, with Harry a discreet distance behind. Yet, although she made an effort to be lighthearted, her thoughts grew heavier as they approached Clavant. Every yard of this route held memories of Kit. Here, where the chalk showed white amongst the tree roots, he had first shown her a badgers' set; in the tangle of brambles a hundred yards on, a willow-wren's nest. What was he doing at this moment, in London, and did he think of her at all? She wondered if he could possibly have heard of Sir Francis's return. Her heart ached for him. If she could but shut her eyes and open them again to find his brown clad figure on the sturdy cob beside her, instead of this elegant young man, however handsome and charming, riding her uncle's best mare.

She sighed unconsciously. Francis turned to her at once. 'You are fatigued?'

'Oh, no. It is nothing.'

'How much further before we sight the house?'

'There is a slope at the end of the wood where one may have an excellent view.'

She led the way through the wood. As they emerged from the trees, she pointed with her whip. 'There it is, the house beside the river.'

He narrowed his eyes. 'It is indeed a pleasant-looking

property. Well watered, sheltered from the wind, not too near the village.'

'And your mother never lived there,' she remarked sadly. 'In fact it is a house without a mistress, even now.'

Again he leaned over and took her hand. 'But it will have, my Phyllida, the most beautiful, desirable mistress in the world.' He glanced around him. 'Let us dismount and walk along this ridge a little way. I grow stiff in the saddle.'

She scarcely considered they had been riding long enough for that, but she forebore to say so. In answer to Francis's raised hand, Harry came forward.

'Walk our horses,' Francis instructed him. 'Miss Marchant and I are strolling to the end of the ridge.'

She saw an odd look in the groom's eyes, anxious, almost alarmed. As Harry tethered his own mount and helped her to dismount, he said very quietly, 'I wouldn't go too far, ma'am, there's quite a keen wind beyond the trees.'

She had never known Harry to offer advice before. She said sharply, 'I am sure Sir Francis will feel the cold before I do.'

Harry shook his head helplessly, and followed behind them, leading the horses as, her hand tucked beneath Francis's arm, they started along the chalky path at the edge of the wood.

Francis turned and said irritably, 'Not this way, you fool. Take the beasts back along the way we have come.'

Harry flushed and said stubbornly, 'Begging your pardon, sir, my orders are not to let Miss Phyllida out of my sight.'

Phyllida was even more astonished at his behaviour. In the past, had he not often flouted those orders and, as soon as she met Kit, taken himself off?

Releasing her arm, Francis faced the groom, his whip

half raised. 'And *my* orders, you insolent fellow, are to do as you are told now, by *me.*'

Harry cast her an appealing glance but she had always been taught that women did not countermand the orders of men. As she moved on, Harry reluctantly turned the horses' heads and walked slowly back along the ridge.

'That is better,' Francis remarked, smiling, as he took her arm again. 'We do not want a servant's prying eyes on us, do we?'

He led her to where the wood thinned; then, glancing over his shoulder, drew her in amongst the trees. Here they were completely hidden both from Harry and the labourers working in the fields below.

'Now, the moment I have been waiting for,' he said, and his voice sounded strangely thick and unfamiliar. He held her wrist and stood looking down at her. His eyes had become suddenly as hard as they had been when she first saw him. 'I do not know whether you are a good actress or merely a fool,' he said in the same tone as he had used yesterday. 'Whichever you are, you must be taught a lesson.'

She said, not understanding this abrupt change, 'But why? What have I done?'

'What have you done? Why, you've cheated me, you wide-eyed innocent-looking chit. I was led to believe you were being guarded like a princess in a tower, with never so much as a look cast at another man. And what do I find? That quite openly, under your guardian's very roof, you have bestowed your favours upon another man. And that man, Glenister, who has already done me sufficient injury. He not only steals my property, but also my future wife. Though, i' faith, the latter could hardly be termed stealing. You appeared so *very* willing.'

She said desperately, 'I do not understand what you are talking about. Mr. Glenister was taken ill yesterday . . .'

'And had you not servants aplenty in the house, that *you* must needs coddle and comfort him? Do not take me for that much of a fool, my dear. A while back you looked quite fearful when you thought I might call out Glenister to make amends, and I do not flatter myself your anxiety was on my behalf. But I have no intention of risking my life, ma'am. It is you, my pretty, who are going to make amends.'

Before she had even realised his intention, he had pulled off her hat, snatched the pins from her hair. She tried to free herself, but he was too strong for her. The charming manner of the past hour had gone completely. In its place was something which brought all her fears back in a rush. They were still nameless. But now the danger, she knew, was very real.

The wood seemed suddenly full of voices, warning voices: Kit's and Lucy's, even Harry's. Francis's face, above her own, became mixed with the memory of his uncle's three years ago. His hands upon her body had the same effect as had Lord Stansted's. What he was doing was wrong, as that had been wrong. Then, she had been helpless. Now, she was not. She raised her free arm and with all her strength cut him across the cheek with her whip.

As he staggered back, she turned and ran, shouting for Harry. She heard Francis's voice behind her.

'You little fool. Come back.'

She paid no heed. There was only fear in the wood now. And the desperate need to escape.

Harry came running, leading Centaur. He cupped his hands for her to mount, thrust her foot into the stirrup, the reins into her hands. He slapped Centaur hard on the flank. As she wheeled the horse, she saw him go down under Francis's furious attack.

Then she was beyond conscious thought. She stretched herself along Centaur's neck as he galloped between the trees. Branches tore at her hair, whipped against her cheeks. Emerging from the wood, the chestnut swerved left and started headlong down the slope to Clavant. Stones and chalk spurted up from his hooves, dust made her eyes smart. Her wrists felt as if they would crack. She knew herself powerless to control the horse. She clung to the pommel and prayed he would not land her in a ditch, or head first on to the sharp stones of the track.

As they reached the village a child ran screaming into a cottage. The geese scattered, hissing, across the green. A labourer ran forward, hand outstretched. Centaur swerved and all but unseated her. Then, ahead, she saw the gates of the manor, wide open. With all her strength she pulled at the chestnut's head. For a few seconds he fought; then slowed, and responded. She galloped up the drive of 'Lady Sarah's house' in a scatter of gravel and came to a rearing halt before the door. She kicked her foot free and slid from the horse and fell against the mounting block, doubled up with the effort of drawing gasping, painful breaths.

She heard the door open behind her. She was beyond any further effort, beyond speech. She expected to find the native servant beside her. Instead, it was Edward Glenister's voice which sounded at her elbow.

'Miss Marchant, what has happened? Has that damned animal bolted and thrown you again?'

She drew breath enough to gasp out, 'No. Yes. I— I . . .' She felt herself swaying. The trees and the house were beginning to fade before her eyes.

'Don't try to talk,' Edward said urgently. 'You're safe now, whatever has happened.'

She was lifted up and carried into the house. His arms were strong about her, and lowered her gently into a deep leather chair before a blazing fire. He put a stool beneath her feet. From a long way away she heard his voice, quietly giving orders.

She said, with a laugh she recognised as bordering on hysteria, 'Kit said to come, if I needed help . . . But I didn't mean to. It was Centaur brought me. Help me, please.'

His face above her was indistinct. But in his eyes she saw the same concern as at their first meeting. His voice came to her from a great distance.

'My dear, I will do anything in the world . . .'

There was no need then for any more striving. She was safe. She ceased to fight against the threatening blackness, and let it envelop her completely.

VII

It took Phyllida some moments, when she regained consciousness, to recall where she was. The room, with its panelled oak walls and shelves of books, was unfamiliar. The heavy desk and leather chairs, the pipe rack and pistol above the mantelpiece all added up to its being a man's room and had no part in her conception of 'Lady Sarah's house'.

Then she saw Edward Glenister, on his knees beside her, chafing her hands. As soon as he saw her eyes open he took a glass from a small table and held it out to her.

'Drink this. But not too fast or it will catch your breath.'

'What is it?'

'Brandy. The best, I assure you. It was smuggled in from France last week.'

She recognised with gratitude that he was talking to put her at ease. Glancing down, she saw that her jacket, which Francis had unfastened, had been buttoned up again. She sipped the brandy, then laid her head against the hard leather of the chair and closed her eyes. She did not want to be brought fully back to the present yet. She did not want to have to answer questions.

She said abstractedly, 'It was like this when we first met. You gave me wine, and I . . .'

'You fell asleep on the grass bank while I caught your horse. Yesterday, we reversed rôles and you came to my rescue.'

She opened her eyes. 'I had forgotten your fever. Are you recovered, so soon?'

'The attacks vary. This one was short and sharp. I would not care to ride fifty miles, but otherwise . . .' He shrugged. 'Take some more brandy, and then, if you feel able to tell me what happened . . . My groom has taken charge of your horse. As I told you before, he is not a fit animal for a young woman to ride.'

She raised her head. 'You will not punish him? It was not his fault this time that he bolted. Harry had . . . Oh, poor Harry.' She sat forward, gripping his sleeve. 'He may be hurt. He came to my aid.'

'You were set upon? Only tell me where this took place, and I will send someone to find your groom.'

'Just inside the wood, at the top of the slope. At least, that was where Sir Francis . . .'

Edward's hand was outstretched to the bell rope. He paused in astonishment. 'Sir Francis was with you? Was he not able to protect you? He is a swordsman of the first order.'

She bit her lip and lowered her eyes, loath to speak the words which would start more questions. She gulped down the brandy too fast and it caught her throat, making her cough. Edward jerked the bell rope.

'Do not distress yourself, Miss Marchant. I will order a search to be made.'

The native servant appeared as silently as before. His face was impassive. Edward spoke to him in his own language and he bowed without speaking and went away.

Phyllida put down her empty glass. 'You have been very kind, Mr. Glenister. I owe you an explanation.'

He shook his head. 'You are not ready to talk yet. Just rest.' He picked up some salve from the little table. 'Miss Marchant, Emma and the ayah have gone for a short drive, my carriage having been mended. My housekeeper is visiting her sister in the village. There is no woman in the house. Will you allow me, therefore, to attend to the cuts on your face?'

He was incredibly gentle, more so than Kit or Henty or even her nurse had been. His face was close to hers. He looked pale and there were hollows under his eyes. The eyes themselves held the same concern as they had when she first saw him. Nothing in his face or his eyes, or the touch of his fingers against her cheek was akin to what had so frightened her up there in the wood with Francis Delaney. This very room, with its wood and leather and masculine quality, seemed like a refuge to her. The warmth of the brandy and the fire spread through her body. Edward's calmness, which had previously so irked her, now helped her to relax.

He put down the salve and sat back on his heels. 'There. Is that more comfortable?'

'Thank you. Yes.' On an impulse which took her unawares, she said, 'Mr. Glenister, I believe that I have wronged you. You did not win this house by gambling, did you?'

He answered at once. 'No. At least, it was not I who gambled.'

'You told me you had come by the property as payment for a debt.'

'That is true. Delaney attempted a private trading venture with an Indian merchant which was unsuccessful. He found himself heavily in debt. I had funds available in India so I put them at his disposal. In return, he made over this property to me.'

There was something in his jerky sentences which troubled her. She said doubtfully, 'But I thought such trading had been stopped when Lord Clive was last in India.'

His face assumed the expression of reserve with which she was now familiar. She added quickly, 'You have no need to—to try to preserve my illusions about Sir Francis. I have every reason now to . . . This transaction he was engaged in was illegal?'

Edward nodded without speaking.

'Then why did you help him, when you so admire Lord Clive and could therefore be expected to carry out his orders?'

He stared into the fire, frowning. As last he said slowly, 'It is probably difficult for you to understand. The British are trying to govern, to bring justice and peace to India. But as yet there are so few of us. What one Englishman does reflects on his compatriots, so that to protect another man's honour is in a way to save one's own.'

He was right. It was difficult to understand. While she was trying to work it out for herself, he turned back to her, smiling.

'You must not think it was an act of great self-sacrifice on my part. It suited me to make the exchange since it is not always easy to transfer one's assets from India to this country.'

'If you had not paid this debt?' she persisted. 'What would have happened to Captain Delaney?'

He stood up and threw another log on the fire. 'You ask too many questions, little Miss Phyllida.'

As always when he used that tone, she was provoked. She said tartly, 'If you had answered them honestly before, I should not have misjudged you.'

He gave her a slight bow. '*Touché.*'

'Why did you let me believe wrongly? Why did you not even attempt to defend yourself?'

His mouth tightened. 'Miss Marchant, I care little for other people's opinions nowadays. When I was younger I was always trying to—to please people. My superiors, the Indian merchants I dealt with, my wife. Most of all, my wife.' He shrugged and spread his hands. 'To what avail? My superiors numbered amongst them men who did their best to break the greatest man India will ever know. The Indian merchants will trick you at every turn. My wife . . .' He shrugged again.

She looked at him in dismay. 'You are so—bitter. I had not thought you bitter. I believe,' she added with sudden perception, 'it is because you have been hurt.'

He clenched his hands and kicked a log further into the hearth. 'You are very young, my dear, and a woman. To you, life is all joy or sorrow. When one is a man and grows older . . .'

'You have neither joy nor sorrow? Kit says I believe what I want to believe. I do not want to believe that. It would make your life so—so empty.'

He swung round to face her, and she knew by his eyes that her instinct was right. She remembered Emma's reference to her father's 'sad look', and to her mother always being cross and tired and not talking to either husband or child. He had been disillusioned, just as she had been. But whereas she would run to Kit or Henty or even Lucy with her hurts, with him it had produced this tightness about the mouth, his air of calm indifference.

He said almost brusquely, 'Life which holds Emma can scarcely be called empty. Miss Marchant, we have spoken enough about myself. I think we should return to your affairs, and that you are now sufficiently recovered to inform me of what actually did befall you in the wood. You were set upon, by highwaymen, foot-pads?'

She turned away, and answered him in a tight, tone-less voice. 'I was set upon, but not by highwaymen.'

'Do you mean to tell me that—*Delaney?*'

She nodded, feeling the blood hot in her cheeks. She saw his hand go to where his sword would be were he carrying one. He swore, then murmured an apology.

'Your guardian allowed you to ride alone with De-laney?'

'Oh yes. He thought it a good idea, that we should get better acquainted.' She drew in her breath sharply, realising the implication, and the truth of Lucy's warn-ing.

Edward persisted in his questions. 'Doubtless Delaney suggested you should dismount and walk a little, and sent your groom away?'

'Yes. It was just like that.'

'And you . . .' He exclaimed in exasperation. 'You have been kept so in ignorance, Kit tells me. You would have no idea. . . . Delaney deserves to be run through with-out mercy, and your guardian. At this moment I could even take a horse whip to your governess.'

For the first time she had seen him roused. The change was so startling she was a little afraid. The knuckles of his hands gleamed whitely, the fair hairs showed clearly on the stretched skin, his brows were drawn together.

The next moment, at the sound of Emma's voice in the hall, he relaxed. The door banged open. The little girl burst into the room, demanding to know what had hap-pened. Her father's figure hid Phyllida from her.

'I have just returned from my drive and I saw Miss Marchant's groom in the yard and his face was all hurt and they told me she was here and—Oh!' Catching sight of Phyllida, she ran forward. 'You are not hurt, ma'am? Please tell me you are not hurt.'

Phyllida embraced the child. 'No, I am not hurt, except for a few scratches. There is no need to be so anxious, darling.'

The little girl clung to her hand. 'What happened? Did your horse run away with you again?'

Edward answered for her. 'Yes, indeed. But he was very clever this time. Instead of throwing Miss Marchant into a bed of nettles he landed her here at our door.'

'And Papa has taken care of you, like you took care of him yesterday?'

'He has taken great care of me. I am quite recovered now, and if Harry is here, I must go home.'

The child's face clouded again. 'Back to that horrid man who was so cross with you yesterday? Why do you not stay here with us? It would be much nicer for you, and make Papa and me very happy.'

Phyllida glanced at Edward, not knowing how to answer. He said quite sternly, 'You are embarrassing Miss Marchant, Emma.'

The little girl looked unhappily from one to the other. 'I do not understand that word, Papa. Have I said something wrong?'

Phyllida laid her hand against the child's cheek. 'No, dear. I wish I could stay with you, but my uncle will be getting anxious if I do not return soon.'

In her heart she knew what the cause of his anxiety would be: that by her action this morning she might again have prejudiced her chance of marrying Francis Delaney. But she was quite certain now that it would take more than a cut across the face with a riding whip to make Francis forgo his chance of her dowry.

She rose, making an attempt to tidy her hair. Edward said, 'If you are sure you are sufficiently recovered, I will fetch my coat and hat and tell them not to put the carriage away.'

'Mr. Glenister, there is no need . . .'

'Yesterday, ma'am, you forbade me to argue with you. Today, I do the same in reverse. You are not fit to ride, and I am certainly not allowing you to face the consequences of this—this incident, alone.'

'I am very grateful to you.' Her immense relief was evident in her voice. She turned to Emma. 'I do not know what you will be able to come again to Meadhayes, dear.'

Emma's mouth drooped. 'Not till that horrid man has gone?'

'Perhaps . . .' She was about to say, 'Perhaps not even then.' But of what use to sadden Emma before it was necessary? She said instead, 'Perhaps it will not be long. You will practise in the meantime?'

'Oh yes, every day.'

When Edward left them, Emma looked searchingly into Phyllida's face. 'You are shaking, ma'am, like Papa was yesterday. But I do not think you have a fever. Were you very frightened when your horse ran away?'

'Yes, very frightened.'

'I think you still are. Is it because of what your uncle will say? You needn't be, you know. Not now Papa is taking you home. He will make it all right. It was only because he was unwell yesterday that he couldn't make it all right then.'

The child's faith in her father reminded Phyllida of Kit, who had told her he trusted Edward Glenister to 'make all things come right in the end'. They both seemed to regard Edward as a magician who could wave a wand and put her world to rights. But he had no more power to do that than she herself. He had not been able to save her from yesterday's humiliation. It was unlikely that he would even gain entry to Meadhayes today. The next encounter with Francis, with Uncle Samuel, was something she had to face alone, and she knew herself helpless before both these men who controlled her future.

Emma was right. She was afraid, far more afraid than if Centaur had truly bolted with her. She sank to her knees and held the child close to her, feeling the warmth of the small body even through her riding suit. Emma put an arm around her neck.

'Don't cry, Miss Phyllida, please don't cry. Papa will look after you, truly he will. See, here he is.'

She hid her face against Emma's, ashamed of her weakness.

Edward said, 'When you are ready, ma'am.'

She was startled by the coldness in his voice. He was standing at the door. His hands were clenched and there was the familiar tightness at the corners of his mouth as if he were holding back some strong emotion. It could have been anger.

Hastily she scrambled to her feet and bade Emma goodbye. 'I am quite ready. It is exceedingly good of you, Mr. Glenister . . .'

His eyes were as cold as his voice. 'Do not exaggerate my goodness, ma'am. There is a limit to every man's control, to what he can endure without weakening his— resolve.'

She stared at him in dismay. What she had done to cause this abrupt change in his manner towards her she could not imagine. Then suddenly, the word 'endure' gave her the clue. Impulsively she laid a hand on his arm.

'I am sorry, sir. I have put an extra burden upon you when you are not fully recovered from your fever. Do you think you *should* venture out? The wind is quite cold.'

He put his hand over hers, his face softening its expression. When he spoke there was a kind of exasperated amusement in his voice.

'My dear little Miss Phyllida, our friend Kit is quite right. You may have learned about herbs and potions and be able to read and write Latin. But of the world, and men, you have no more knowledge than Emma.'

The journey to Chichester seemed to Phyllida both too short and too long. Too short because every mile they covered brought her nearer to the inevitable meetings with Uncle Samuel and Francis Delaney. Too long because she was again ill at ease with the man sitting opposite her. That last remark before they left the manor had caused a return of the self-consciousness which had plagued her on her first formal visit to the house. She had wanted to argue, to demand of him how she could help being ignorant if nobody would enlighten her. But such an outburst had seemed in itself childish, so she had kept silent.

Whereas at the time it had seemed the most natural thing in the world to accept his offer to accompany her home, she was now very conscious of the impropriety of such behaviour. True, Harry was riding behind, leading Centaur. The fact remained that she was alone in a carriage with a man to whom she was in no way related, a man whom her guardian had caused to be thrown from his house.

She shrank back in the corner, hoping she might not be seen, wondering if Francis had returned to Mead-hayes and if so, what tale he had told.

Edward appeared as much preoccupied with his thoughts as she was. From his expression as he stared out of the window, they seemed equally troublesome. Or perhaps, she reflected, it was that he was feeling unwell.

At last he turned to her. 'Miss Marchant, I surmise that after what has happened this morning, you are more than ever opposed to the idea of marriage to Delaney.'

'I—I dread the thought of it.'

'You have no further need to be anxious on that score. It will not take place.'

She sat forward. 'What did you say?'

'It is a marriage which cannot be allowed,' he said firmly. 'I intend to prevent it, this very day.'

She exclaimed incredulously, 'You cannot know what you are saying. There is no possible way . . .'

'There is a way. But you have no need to know what means I shall use. Let it be sufficient that you rest assurd you will be free of this man who, I think you now recognize, could bring you nothing but unhappiness. More than that, I cannot promise.'

'*More* than that?' she echoed. 'What could be more welcome to me than to be free of that odious man?'

'Is it not your heart's desire to marry Kit Burrell?'

'Yes. Oh, yes. But even were I freed of the obligation to marry Sir Francis, Uncle Samuel would never allow me to marry Kit.'

'That is what I mean,' he said regretfully. 'If the marriage with Delaney does not take place—which it will not, I do assure you—I do not know what Mr. Gunter's position will be. Delaney has brought this situation on himself. But what attitude Lord Stansted will take . . . You are, I assume, fully aware by now of the circumstances of your betrothal?'

She answered bitterly, 'Fully aware. Kit explained quite clearly I was not more than a saleable asset in my guardian's eyes.'

Edward raised his eyebrows. 'It could have been more kindly expressed. However, we both know that young Burrell is a stickler for the truth.'

Feeling her way, she asked, 'You think that Uncle Samuel in those circumstances would lose his position on the Court of Directors of the East India Company?'

'It will depend, I think, on whom Lord Stansted vents his anger. He is a man without principles, as witness his attack upon Lord Clive. To him and to your guardian, money is of paramount importance—money, and power. And Lord Stansted has the power to have your guardian removed.'

She was out of her depth, and told him so.

'Naturally,' he said. 'Politics, economics, wars, are not for women to trouble their heads about. It is sufficient that they confine themselves to perfecting the talents with which they are endowed.'

She experienced the familiar irritation with his superior attitude. 'You do not approve of a woman being educated?'

'I did not say that. If she enjoys learning, as you obviously do, I would greatly encourage it. But politics and affairs of business are mostly conducted in a manner few women would understand. A woman is guided by her loves and hates . . .'

She thought, That is true. She had been guided in her judgment of him by the hurt she believed him to have done her.

She asked, with sudden intuition, 'Your wife did not enjoy learning?'

He sighed heavily. 'There was little she did enjoy, I fear, either inside or outside the home.'

'Not even Emma's company? I find the hours spent with her most enjoyable. She is so very lively and gay and affectionate.' She bit her lip. 'I should not have said that, I think. It implied criticism of your wife, and she is dead.'

'She was too unwell or fatigued most of the time to endure Emma's chatter. I suppose I have indulged the child. I fear the excellent Miss Henty thinks so.'

'Hen is very strict,' Phyllida said feelingly. 'That, I think, is why you are able to accuse me of childishness. I have scarce been allowed out of her sight, even when I have been with other young ladies. That was why I needed to escape, to be with Kit who was not always finding fault.'

'Yet she has affection for you, I am sure. Her strictness has been, I surmise, directed towards your own good in her eyes.'

'And great good it has done me,' she flared. 'Look what happened today, for instance.'

'You are right. For that, I cannot forgive her.'

'At least it has determined me in one thing.'

'What is that?'

She did not answer. Only to herself did she resolve that at the first opportunity she would force Lucy to answer her questions and put an end to ignorance.

She saw with dismay that they were passing the alms houses just outside the city wall. She made another attempt to tidy her hair, but without pins or a filet there was little she could do. Her palms felt clammy inside her gloves and her heart began to beat uncomfortably fast.

Edward leaned across and took her hand. 'Do not distress yourself. You have nothing to fear.'

'If he is already there—Sir Francis, I mean?'

'I will deal with him. You need not even see him. Go straight to your room and ring for your maid or Miss Henty.'

'Uncle Samuel will be sure to send for me.'

'He is abed with the gout, you told me.'

'Oh, yes.' She sighed with relief. 'Perhaps he will not be well enough to be disturbed. But he cannot have the gout for ever,' she added ruefully.

He pressed her fingers. 'Phyllida, he cannot harm you. Doubtless he will be angry. But you are not without a certain rebelliousness which you can call to your aid when necessary.' He smiled suddenly, the smile which made him look ten years younger. 'Try answering him in Latin. That will confound him.'

She made an attempt to match his smile. But they were turning into the stable yard and she felt cold and, despite his presence, terribly alone.

He said earnestly, 'You do not believe I can save you from Delaney, do you?'

She faced him, taut with self-control. 'No. I am sorry. Short of running him through with a sword, of which you spoke an hour since, I can think of no possible way . . .'

'My dear Miss Phyllida, if there were no other means, I would willingly duel with him on your behalf. But Dasim Ali and I, between us, will set you free this very day, I trust, and it will not be with a sword.'

She did not, dared not, believe him. He was lying, as all men lied, it seemed, save Kit.

So far, it had all been easier than Phyllida had anticipated. Francis had not yet showed up at Meadhayes. Uncle Samuel had not left his room, and this being on the opposite side of the house to the stable yard, he had not even heard Edward's carriage, or the horses returning. Miss Henty was up and dressed, looking pale and drawn, and had been primed by Edward with the story of the runaway horse. She had insisted that Phyllida go straight to bed and had herself given Samuel Gunter the news, adding that Harry had saved Phyllida unknown to Sir Francis who had presumably become lost while searching for her in countryside he was not acquainted with.

Samuel Gunter had accepted this story, agreed with the governess that Phyllida should remain in bed for the rest of the day, and given orders that Centaur should be shot.

Horrified, Phyllida defied Miss Henty and leaned out of the window in her dressing wrapper, making signals to Harry that he should shoot into the air so that her uncle would believe his instructions had been carried out.

'I will take the blame,' she called down as he came to stand below her side window. 'Oh, your poor face, Harry! Does it hurt greatly?'

' 'Tis nothing, ma'am—not nearly so deep a cut as you give Sir Francis.'

'I have had no chance as yet to thank you for coming to my aid.'

'That I stayed within earshot was thanks to Lucy, ma'am. She guessed what was a'coming.'

Phyllida had not wanted to go to bed. Now that she was there, with a hot brick at her feet and a tray of food beside her while Henty and Lucy fussed over her, she felt suddenly drained of strength, thankful that no more effort was needed from her this day. But there was one matter she was determined to settle, tired as she felt. When the governess went downstairs for a meal, Phyllida ordered Lucy to lock her bedroom door on the inside.

'Whatever for, ma'am? Sir Francis wouldn't dare come up here.'

'Do as I say and don't ask questions.'

Wide-eyed, the maid obeyed her.

'Now hand me the key.'

Reluctantly, Lucy complied.

'Now,' said Phyllida firmly, 'You are not leaving this room until you have answered my questions. I refuse any longer to be kept in ignorance of what is expected of me when I marry Sir Francis.'

For she was quite sure the marriage would take place. This time she was not prepared to accept what she would dearly like to believe; that Edward Glenister could wave a magician's wand and prevent it.

Edward pulled his chair closer to the drawing-room

fire, rang for Dasim Ali and ordered a bottle of claret. The drive to Chichester and back in the cold wind, the long wait in the notary's office, had done him no good. It would be infuriating if the fever laid hold of him again just as he needed to be fully active, with all his wits about him. He moved a piece on the chess-board beside him, then frowned, recognising what a foolish move it had been.

Dasim Ali stood by his chair, proffering a filled glass. 'You are unwell, sahib?'

'I think the malaria has not left me completely.'

'You should go to bed.'

Edward shook his head. 'I am expecting a messenger from the notary. I went to collect the statement I obtained from the Reverend Mr. Wilkinson, but the lawyer was out of town and the clerk did not know where to find it.'

'Why did you not keep Mr. Wilkinson's letter here, sahib?'

'I deemed it safer lodged with a lawyer. He had my instructions that, in the event of my death, he was to present it to Mr. Gunter should Miss Marchant's marriage to Sir Francis Delaney appear imminent.'

The servant's nostrils narrowed. 'Papers. Statements,' he said scornfully. 'That is not the way of my people.'

'I know,' Edward said feelingly. 'You take the law into your own hands.'

'It is the best way, sahib. You do not know that this method is certain.'

'Nevertheless, it is the one I propose to use.'

'I know a better.'

Edward glanced up quickly. 'Murder, I suppose?'

The butler nodded. His dark eyes gleamed, his beard jutted forward. 'Is there not murder in your own heart, sahib?'

Edward moved uneasily in his chair. 'Possibly. But not in my head.'

'With me, the head will obey the heart.' His voice took on an urgent note. 'It must not be allowed to happen, sahib. The memsahib is very young and beautiful. To be married to *that* man would . . .'

'I am well aware of what would happen, Dasim Ali. That, as you know, is why I wrote to Mr. Wilkinson.'

'You think they will accept that letter?'

'Of course. He is a minister of the church and he had witnesses. And there is your own evidence.'

The servant's lips curled, his nostrils narrowed again. 'They will not take heed of anything I say, sahib. In England I am regarded as a savage. It is well, I think, that I behave as one.'

Edward frowned. 'Dasim Ali, do you know the penalty for killing a man in this country?'

The butler nodded impassively, 'A man has to die one way or the other. I would consider it an honour to be hanged that you might have the memsahib for yourself.'

Edward slammed down his glass so that the wine spilled over. 'That is not what I have in mind at all.'

The thick black eyebrows lifted, the dark eyes expressed doubt.

Edward said quickly, 'Miss Marchant wishes to marry someone else. Though why I should discuss this matter with you, I cannot conceive.'

The servant put his palms together and bowed. 'I have offended?'

'No,' Edward exclaimed impatiently. 'You have but touched me on the raw.'

'Sahib?'

'It is an English expression, you would not understand.'

'No, sahib, I do not understand at all. You desire a woman. A man stands in your way. I kill him for you.

Afterwards you take this woman, beget a son on her and she will soon forget this other man. It is simple.' He spread his hands in a gesture which implied that the matter was already settled.

'Simple!' Edward put his head in his hands. 'Dasim Ali, I envy you.'

The Indian's soft voice was calmly reasonable. 'You are troubled by what your countrymen call honour, sahib. It means, I have been taught, keeping your word to your fellow men. I have not understood that it has anything to do with women.'

Edward lifted his head and studied the servant's face. The East in distance and time was half a world away. But it was in this room, here beside him. He recalled the hopelessness he had felt at trying to make contact with the Indians, the amazement and derision of the English colony in Madras that he should even try. He could hear Ellen's voice even now.

'You make yourself a laughing stock, Edward, treating the natives as if they were human beings like ourselves. One day you will suffer for it, you'll see.'

He drained his glass of claret. 'Your ways are not mine, Dasim Ali. I appreciate your wish to help me. But I will manage this affair my own way. You understand?'

Again the act of submission; the palms pressed together, the grave bow, the lowered eyes.

'You may go, Dasim Ali.'

The servant moved silently across the room. The door opened and shut without a sound. It was almost as if a ghost had passed out of the room. Edward shivered, although he was not now feeling cold. The very atmosphere seemed charged with the mystery, the unpredictability of the East. Unpredictable, save in their attitude towards women. 'Beget a son on her . . .'

He shifted in his chair. Ever since this morning he had been haunted by the sight of Phyllida on her knees, holding Emma so closely to her while tears glistened on her lashes. Not once had he seen Ellen show such affection, even for her own daughter. Nor would Emma ever have dared put her arm around her mother's neck and kissed her in that wholly spontaneous manner. He had been so moved that he had been forced to clench his hands against the desire to embrace this girl who loved his child, to enfold them both within his own arms. He had forced harshness into his voice in case it should betray his real feelings.

He stood up and began to pace the room. Dasim Ali's voice was in the air all about him.

'You desire a woman.'

So it was obvious to his servant, even if she herself had not the least suspicion. Of course he desired her. He had done so from the very beginning, when she lay sleeping at the edge of the downland track. This morning, when he carried her inside his house, when she was actually in his arms . . . And yesterday . . . Then, he reminded himself bitterly, he had caught a glimpse of what might have been. He had seen the woman behind the girl, recognised the strength of which she herself was probably not aware, been shown a tenderness which Ellen had never once offered in their time together. In those few moments before her guardian and Delaney had burst in on them, she had revealed herself to him with as little reserve as she did to Emma. As she did to young Burrell?

He kicked savagely at a log in the hearth. What was it Dasim Ali had said? 'Afterwards you take this woman, beget a son on her and she will soon forget this other man. It is simple.'

Simple? To take advantage of her gratitude when he had freed her from Delaney? To take advantage of young Burrell's absence? To play upon her feelings by revealing the unhappiness of his marriage, by using

Emma's affection for her as extra pressure? Oh yes, it would be simple enough, no doubt, provided he could overcome her guardian's opposition. Even that might prove possible, if he offered to forgo her dowry. How had she described herself? 'A saleable asset'. If the sale to one man proved impossible, might not her guardian give her away to another, knowing her provided for, for the rest of her days?

Where would it get him in the end? Edward demanded of himself fiercely. Another marriage beset by his self-condemnation, by knowing he had brought unhappiness to a second woman. And what would it do to Phyllida? She had suffered disillusion at the hands of her guardian and Delaney. Was he to add his own selfishness to theirs, exchange one unacceptable husband for another? No, that was not being fair to himself. He was not Delaney. He would never harm her, hurt her. Wouldn't he? truth demanded of him. By freeing her, and then standing between her and the young man to whom she had given her heart long since, he would be dealing her another cruel blow. And he had the audacity to tell himself he loved her.

He picked up the half empty glass, twirled it in his fingers, staring at the swirling liquid. Then he hurled it against the wall. It splintered into tiny fragments. Over the new flock wallpaper a red stain spread, like blood, he thought, and shivered again. He cursed himself for a superstitious fool, and Dasim Ali for being the voice of temptation.

It was almost dark when the notary's messenger arrived. The package was brought to Edward by the new parlourmaid.

'Give the fellow this,' he said, 'and thank him for his trouble. Then come and clear up this mess. I—I had an accident with my wine glass.'

He saw the maid's gaze travel from the broken glass

on the floor to the stain on the wall, then to the bottle on the table beside his chair. She bobbed a curtsey and hurried from the room.

He read the parson's statement through as she was sweeping up, although he knew the words by heart. Then he asked, 'Is the fire still alight in the library?'

The maid looked up nervously. 'No, sir. I didn't know you . . .'

'It does not matter. I can as well deal with this here. Send Dasim Ali to me and tell him to bring my writing materials.'

'I do not know where to find him, sir,' she stammered.

Edward frowned. 'He must be somewhere in the house.'

'No, sir.'

'What do you mean, no?'

'He—he went out, sir.'

'I did not give him permission to do so. How long ago was this?'

'About an hour, sir.'

He stared at the girl, nervously brushing at a floor already clear of glass splinters. Above her head the wine stain showed darkly red in the candlelight.

'Go and find out if any of the horses are missing,' he ordered. 'At once.'

The girl was back within minutes, her eyes large in her white face. 'One of the carriage horses has been took, sir.'

Again it seemed to Edward that the East had come into this English drawing-room.

'A man has to die one way or the other. I would consider it an honour to be hanged that you might have the memsahib for yourself. A man stands in your way. I kill him for you. It is simple.'

He was being a fool, he told himself. Dasim Ali had merely gone off on some secret affair of his own. Without permission, and taking a horse into the bargain? Dasim Ali, who had never once in his three years of service disobeyed an order, nor given a moment's cause for anxiety? And what secret affair could he have in Chichester or anywhere else in this neighbourhood where he had declared himself regarded as a savage?

Edward sprang to his feet. 'Don't stand gaping there, girl. Fetch my boots and riding cape, and tell Tom to have my mare saddled at once.'

He flung past her into the hall, caught up his sword belt and fastened it on, telling himself even as he did so that he was being melodramatic, that the fever was still on him, blurring common sense. But he had to make sure.

He strode into the library. There was still sufficient light from the dying fire to do without a candle. In England he no longer slept with his pistol beside his bed. For want of a better place he had balanced it on two struts above the mantelpiece. He reached up his hand, then paused, staring in disbelief. He found a candle, stirred the fire into life and lit the wick. Holding it high, he stared again at the wall above the mantelpiece. The wall was bare.

VIII

Phyllida could no longer remain in bed. She had dozed for a while, with Henty sitting beside her. But now, with the sky darkening above the rooftops opposite, a restlessness laid hold of her. When the governess went downstairs for supper, she got out of bed and walked about the room, fiddling with ornaments, opening and shutting drawers to no purpose. She emptied the contents of her jewel box on the bed and examined them, piece by piece, without really noting the precious stones she held in her hands.

She was relieved when Lucy appeared. The maid's face was flushed, her eyes bright.

'Oh, ma'am, I've got news.'

'Well?'

'Sir Francis has returned to the hostelry. He rode in an hour ago and the ostler brought the master's horse round here—in a terrible condition so Harry says. And the ostler told Harry . . .' She paused to make sure of Phyllida's full attention. 'He told Harry that Sir Francis had to be helped from the saddle. Drunk he was, blind drunk. And,' she went on hurriedly before Phyllida could speak, 'I've a bit more to tell yet. Harry—and I never knew he had it in him—has been up to the master's room and told him that if the horse is ruined, he won't be held responsible. And the master went to the window and Harry led the poor beast round for him to see for himself. Mr. Gunter fair lifted the roof with his language, so William said, who was in the bedroom at the time. Well, you know what the master's like about horses, ma'am. If an animal's wrong, 'tis shot. If 'tis right, it's mollycoddled more than a sick child.'

Phyllida said thoughtfully, 'So my uncle is angry with Sir Francis?'

'Angry isn't the word for it, Miss Phyllida. He's that blazing mad William says he's like to have a seizure. And what's he doing now but dressing, and vowing he's going round to the Dolphin and Anchor to give Sir Francis a piece of his mind.'

Phyllida stared at the jade necklace dangling from her fingers. In the fading light the links of the gold chain glinted, the stones looked dark as pine trees. It had always been her favourite, and there were plenty to choose from. She had appreciated and been gratified by the jewels, the gowns and luxuries lavished upon her by Uncle Samuel. But in the end, did she mean any more to him than the best mount in his Sussex stables? If he had been told the truth of what had happened in the wood this morning, would he have raged and stormed and risen from his bed to take Sir Francis to task? She knew the answer only too well. Uncle Samuel had nothing to lose by confronting Francis over his treatment of an animal. By complaining about Francis's treatment of herself, he stood to lose a very great deal.

She dropped the necklace into the jewel box and slammed down the lid.

'Lucy, open the window.'

'The night air is dangerous, ma'am.'

'I will risk it. I feel stifled in here. Bring me my cloak to put around my shoulders.'

The maid did as she was told, then stood beside Phyllida at the window. 'What is it, ma'am? I thought you'd be pleased to know the master is in such a pet with Sir Francis.'

'It will make no difference in the long run, Lucy. The fact is that I am very troubled in my mind.'

'Yes, ma'am, I can understand that,' the maid said sympathetically. 'Especially now you know what Sir Francis was about, and what you can expect from him.'

'I was not referring to that. It is—something connected with Mr. Glenister. He assured me . . .'

'Yes, ma'am?' The maid's face was eager, expectant.

Phyllida said slowly, 'He assured me that he would be able to prevent my marriage to Captain Delaney.'

Lucy clasped her hands together. 'Oh, Miss Phyllida! But how?'

'That is the point. There is no possible way that I can think of. Why do men invent such lies, Lucy?'

' 'Tis part of their nature. They don't always intend to, I think. Some of them just get carried away, like, wanting to impress you. But why should Mr. Glenister invent a lie about a thing like that?'

'That is what troubles me. I cannot believe him. Yet,

as you ask, why should he pretend he can do this for me? In any case, why should he want to?'

'Well, as to that . . .' The maid broke off, twisting her apron between her stubby fingers. 'No, 'tis best I keep silent. Didn't he give you any notion of how he was going to stop the marriage, ma'am?'

'None whatever. He said there was no need for me to know the method. It should suffice that I rest assured it could be done.'

'Then I'd believe him. He's a gentleman who knows what he's about, that I'll wager. *And* wouldn't let much stand in his way neither to my way o' thinking. Now don't you fret, miss. I shouldn't be surprised if he made everything come all right, by some means we can't even guess at.'

There it was again, the fantastic notion that this man was somehow superhuman and could work miracles. Kit, Emma, and now Lucy. They all had this faith in Edward Glenister. She could not share it; dared not, in case of yet another disappointment.

She gazed down into the street. It was almost dark now, but she could recognise the faces of some of the passers-by. Two young clerks, coming from the Council chamber along the street, shared a joke noisily. A farm wagon trundled heavily over the cobbles. A group of urchins raced past, leaping back and forth over the central gutter.

Phyllida sighed, wishing she were a man so that she could venture out alone, into the noise and bustle of the town. Henty considered it unnatural, this desire of hers to be unfettered, free to come and go as she pleased. No other young lady she had ever had charge of, the governess averred, had expressed such an unfeminine notion.

She was about to turn away from the window when

something caught her eye across the way. She leaned forward.

'Lucy, is that a man hiding in the shadows beside Mr. Bolting's house?'

The maid peered out, her mouth open in concentration. 'It is that, ma'am. Now I wonder which of the servant girls he's waiting for.'

Phyllida sat back. 'Is that all he is doing? I had a fancy he might be a footpad.'

'You're being fanciful again, Miss Phyllida. You know we don't have such folks in this part of Chichester. What chance would a footpad have here, with all the houses, and so many people about to catch him?'

'You are right. But he does appear furtive. Look, he has moved a little and—Lucy!' She gripped the maid's arm. 'I could have sworn that he . . .'

' 'Tis a black man, with a queer headgear, and a thick beard.'

'So I thought. It is surely Mr. Glenister's Indian servant. What could he be doing here at this hour?'

'Perhaps he's come with a message.'

'In that case, why does he not deliver it? Oh, there is Uncle Samuel coming from his room.'

A door crashed open along the passage. Her guardian's heavy footsteps sounded on the landing, uneven, punctuated by grunts. The gout was apparently still troubling him. Phyllida held her breath until he reached the hall.

'Mind he don't see you at the window, ma'am,' Lucy warned. 'Especially with it open.'

'He will not look up here.' Phyllida turned her attention again to the street below, and the shadowy figure across the way. It had grown dark now. House and gate lanterns had been lit, throwing pools of light on to the cobbles. A man was making his way uncertainly up the street, surrounded by the pack of urchins who jeered and taunted but kept carefully out of range of his drawn sword.

Lucy began to laugh. ' 'Tis as good as a peepshow, standing here.' Then her tone changed. 'Oh, goodness, ma'am. Do you see who that gentleman is?'

'Yes, I see,' Phyllida answered grimly. 'It is Captain Delaney. And, as you told me, he is very drunk. Lucy, do you not think we should warn Uncle Samuel? If he starts upbraiding Sir Francis, and he in that state and with his sword out . . . Please go down at once.'

The maid screwed up her apron. 'I daren't, miss, not with the master in such a rage already.'

'Then *I* will. However unkindly Uncle Samuel has treated me, I cannot let him . . .'

'It's too late, ma'am. There's the front door opening and . . . Oh-h!' The exclamation was long-drawn, horrified.

Phyllida, half-way across the room, swung round. 'What is it?'

'Look, ma'am—the black man.'

Across the way, Dasim Ali had stepped from the shadows. Clearly, in the light of a lantern, Phyllida saw the heavy pistol in his hand. Equally clearly, above the street noises, she heard his voice, low and calm.

'Captain Delaney, sahib.'

Francis paused, then turned uncertainly towards the speaker. The native servant raised his hand, took aim. Francis started forward, sword arm raised. He tottered, lurched sideways.

The flash momentarily blinded Phyllida. The explosion crashed and reverberated along the street. When she opened her eyes, smoke hung in the air. Through it she could see that Francis was still on his feet. But on the path just inside the gate of Meadhayes, Uncle Samuel lay on his face. A dark stain was spreading slowly on to the cobbles.

By the time Phyllida had recovered her senses and rushed downstairs, the servants had laid Samuel Gunter on a couch in the drawing-room. They clustered around him, scared, uncertain what to do, while a crowd gathered outside the front door. She heard the cries of 'Murder. A savage. Vengeance.' Then she was bending over her guardian, appalled at what she saw.

The ball had entered his chest above the heart and lodged, she felt sure, in his lung. Blood had soaked through shirt and waistcoat. He was breathing in short gasps and coughing spasmodically. There was blood upon his lips.

For horrified seconds Phyllida stared down at him, as helpless as the servants. In her extremity, she called silently on Kit. 'Help me. Help me to know what to do.'

It was as if he stood beside her, calming her, restoring her senses. She straightened and gave precise orders.

'Send Harry for Dr. Burrell. Lucy, fetch linen. William, undo his waistcoat and help me sit him up a little so that he may breathe more easily.'

Impatiently she flung off the cloak which impeded her movements. Snatching the linen from Lucy, she folded it into a pad and pressed it over the wound. Striving to save her guardian's life, she was only half aware of what was happening about her. She heard Harry shouting above the noise in the street, urging the crowd to let him through. She saw Henty slide to the floor in a faint. She heard a wavering, high-pitched laugh in the hall and Francis Delaney's voice, blurred by drink.

She said, without looking up, 'Send him away.'

William went quietly from the drawing-room. There was a scuffle in the hall. The candles flickered in the draught from the door. Then it was closed, the bolts shot. The noise from the street was muffled a little by the window shutters. But even in her concentration

Phyllida recognised that the cries of the crowd had taken on a different note, had become a concentrated roar. It reminded her of the audience at a bear-baiting, or the baying of hounds approaching the kill. There was a shrill scream, then silence. After a moment the uproar started again, though different in tone now, almost triumphant. She could even hear laughter punctuating the shouts.

Then she was aware only of Uncle Samuel's voice.

'Phyllida?' he whispered.

'I am here. Lie still.'

His eyes opened. 'I'm—done for, aren't I?'

She strove to keep her voice steady. 'No, of course not. Harry has gone for Dr. Burrell, he will . . .'

'It was that Indian servant of Glenister's, wasn't it? I caught a glimpse of him just before . . . Why should he want to murder me?'

'The shot was not meant for you, sir. It was intended for Captain Delaney. I pray you do not try to talk, the effort is too much.'

He closed his eyes and remained silent for a few minutes while she pressed the pad against the wound, trying to staunch the bleeding, and prayed that the doctor would come swiftly. The sweat stood out on her guardian's forehead, the waxy blue colour of his face frightened her. She motioned to William to wipe the blood from his lips. He began to speak again in short jerky sentences.

'He intended—to kill Delaney—you said? You—knew about it, then? Planned it, probably—with Glenister.'

'No! Oh, no!' She was appalled by the suggestion. 'I saw from my window . . . Oh, please, Uncle Samuel, try to keep quiet . . .'

His eyes opened wide and focussed on her face. The expression in them made her shrink back.

'You'd have me . . . keep quiet . . . of course,' he

gasped. 'Because . . .' Another spasm of coughing stopped him. The blood that the footman wiped from his lips was now a frothy red. Determinedly he fought for breath. His words sounded clearly above the clatter of hooves in the street, the voice of Dr. Burrell shouting to be let through the crowd.

'You—and Glenister—planned to murder Delaney because—because Glenister is your lover.'

Phyllida heard the servants' gasps of dismay. Lucy exclaimed indignantly, 'It's not true, sir! It's not true!'

Phyllida was incapable of uttering a word. The accusation was so monstrously untrue that she could scarcely believe he could have uttered it.

Her guardian drew a long, gurgling breath, coughed feebly. The blood frothed at the corners of his mouth. His head fell sideways.

The candles flickered again. Dr. Burrell's heavy tread sounded across the hall. His voice shattered the quiet of the room.

'Miss Marchant, I came as quickly as I could.'

'Yes, Doctor Burrell, I am sure you did.' Her voice seemed unnaturally calm. She stood up and faced him, the blood-soaked linen pad still in her hands. 'You are, nevertheless, too late.'

The calmness was momentary. She began to shake uncontrollably. Sobs tore at her throat. She dropped the pad and put her hands to her face; then, feeling the wetness on her cheeks, drew them away abruptly and stared at her red fingers.

'I—I could not save him,' she blurted out between sobs. 'But—worse than that. He thought me—he thought me . . .'

She was gathered into Lucy's arms. The maid's voice was rough with pity. 'There, there, Miss Phyllida, don't you fret. The master didn't know what he was saying. You've nothing to reproach yourself with, every one of us knows that. And so would the master have done if he'd not been so far gone. Don't give another thought to his words, my pretty.'

Lucy led her from the drawing-room and along the hall into the parlour. The fire had been poked into life, a pair of candles lit upon the mantelpiece. In the flickering light Phyllida saw a man standing before the hearth in Uncle Samuel's favourite position. For one wild moment she thought he had returned to life. Trembling, she buried her face against Lucy's shoulder.

'There, there, my pet,' the maid soothed. 'You've no need to take on so. 'Tis Mr. Glenister, not Sir Francis.'

Phyllida raised her head. Edward stepped forward and bowed gravely.

'Miss Marchant, I cannot express . . .'

'How did you get in?' she demanded.

'Your governess invited me to wait in here.'

She heard the shrillness in her voice as she repeated, 'Invited you? Into this house, at such a time? And how does it happen that you are here at all?'

'I came after Dasim Ali, as swiftly as I could.'

'To make sure he had carried out your orders? And now you find he has shot the wrong man. How will you punish him for such a stupid mistake?'

He said heavily, 'Dasim Ali has already been dealt with, by the crowd.' There was a terrible bitterness in his voice. 'He would have approved of that. He did not hold with trials and statements and being confined in gaols.'

She drew in her breath sharply, remembering the sound in the street that was like that at a bear-baiting; the scream, the cries of triumph.

'You sent him to that?' she exclaimed. 'You ordered him to shoot Captain Delaney, fully aware of what would happen to him? I see now why you told me you would not fight a duel. There would have been danger in that for you. Instead, you forced a servant who was devoted to you, so Emma declared . . .' She broke off, clutching at Lucy as his figure began to waver before her eyes.

He said evenly, 'Miss Marchant, you are naturally very distraught. Will you not sit down and let your maid fetch a rug or something warm to put around you?'

She was suddenly aware of her appearance. The front of her dressing wrapper was blood-stained, and her hands and arms. Her hair hung loose on her shoulders. She sank into the chair beside the hearth and huddled into the corner away from the light, while Lucy ran from the room.

Edward went on his knees beside her and began to chafe her hands as he had done that morning. 'Miss Phyllida, I would not have had this happen for the world.'

She could not control her trembling. Her teeth chattered as if she had a fever. She snatched her hands from his grasp.

'Do not lie to me any more. You told me this very morning that you would free me from the necessity to marry Sir Francis, but I must not question you as to the method you would use. You said—and I remember your very words—"Dasim Ali and I between us will set you free this very day, and it will not be with a sword." Not a sword, but a pistol! Not a duel, but a shot, in cold blood! It is true I longed to be free of Sir Francis. But not this way. Not by murder.'

'I do assure you . . .' he began.

'What do you assure me? That you had no knowledge of what your servant was about? Why then did you come? Or did you *happen* to be passing along North Street at this time?'

'I told you, I came after Dasim Ali. I knew well enough . . .'

'There! You have admitted it, you see.'

He rose as Lucy returned with cloak and rugs. The fire was burning more brightly now and Phyllida's dishevelled appearance more obvious. Hastily the maid covered her up.

Lucy said diffidently, 'Sir, I think perhaps you should not be here, not with Miss Phyllida not properly dressed, like.'

He sighed and said wearily, 'You are right. I should not have come at all, not so soon. I hoped I might be of some service. As it is, I can but say again that if it were possible to blot out the last hour from our lives . . .'

'And have it over again?' Phyllida demanded. 'And so make sure that your servant aimed aright and killed the man intended instead of . . .' Her voice broke. She buried her face in her hands. 'Do you know what you have done? You have caused the death of the only person in the world on whom I have the slightest claim. You have ended my life, as well as Uncle Samuel's.'

Lucy said quite sharply, 'Now, now, Miss Phyllida, that's foolish talk.'

She did not care if it was. She was at the end of her strength. The horror of the last half-hour came back to her. Again in her ears sounded her guardian's accusation. She raised her head and looked straight at Edward.

'Do you really expect me to believe that a native servant would venture into Chichester by night on his own account, to shoot an English officer, and with no thought of escaping afterwards?'

He answered sadly, 'Whether you believe it or not, it is true.'

'But why? Why should he do such a foolhardy thing?'

'If I told you the reason, you would not believe that either.'

'Then you had best keep silent, had you not?'

He turned away from her, picked up hat and whip. 'I will go now. I see that my presence here is only causing you more distress. However, I will venture to leave this with you.' He drew from his pocket a folded paper and laid it on the small table beside her. 'When you are calmer, I pray you read it carefully. And try to believe that it was the weapon, the only weapon, that I intended to use against Captain Delaney.'

'A sheet of paper?' she demanded scornfully.

'Yes. Just that.'

Fervently she wished he would become angry, make some excuse, however flimsy, for what he had done. Instead, there was the same unruffled calmness. And as before, it provoked her into a furious outburst.

'Go, I pray you, go. And never come near this house again. As for this . . .' She sat forward, clutching the cloak tightly to her, and reached for the document he had left on the table.

Just in time he saw her intention. Stooping swiftly, he caught the paper within six inches of the flames.

'Ah, no. That I cannot allow. Though you may think the blackest thoughts of me and wish never to set eyes on me again, I insist that in due time you read this paper. For it still affects your future. I will leave it in the safe hands of your governess.'

He went from her, his tread like that of an old man. The door closed softly behind him. Phyllida stared at it for a few seconds, still seeing his face, the sadness of it, the weariness which made him look the thirty-five she had first thought him. Added to grief and shock now was a terrible hurt for which she had no name. The walls of the room began to waver, and it was not due to the flicker of the flames and candles. Before the darkness engulfed her completely, she heard her own voice, as if from a far distance, crying out desperately.

'Lucy, I cannot be mistaken, can I? Tell me that I have not wronged him again.'

Long, long afterwards, it seemed, she found herself in her bed, a hot brick at her feet, the fire lit in the little grate, and Henty sitting beside her. For a moment she thought she might have had another nightmare, that the horror she had been through was only another dreadful dream.

Then she saw the governess' face. It struck her for the first time that Henty must be quite old. Even in her own distress, as the possibility that it was all a dream faded, she felt a stab of pity. What now would happen to Henty? What would happen to them all, now that Uncle Samuel was dead?

The governess bent over her. 'That is better, child.' Her voice was very gentle.

'I do not remember,' Phyllida began. 'Not after Mr. Glenister . . .'

'You fainted, which is not to be wondered at. When you came to, Dr. Burrell gave you a strong potion. You have slept for some hours.'

'Should I not have been praying?' she asked guiltily.

'You had come to the end of your strength. For two days now you have been under the greatest strain. You must rest, child. Try to sleep again. No more can be done until daylight. But first, I wish to read you this.'

'What is it?'

'The document Mr. Glenister left with me.'

Phyllida turned her head on the pillow. 'I do not want to hear.'

Miss Henty's voice resumed its normal decisive tone. 'Nevertheless you will listen. No, Phyllida, you are not to stop up your ears. If you do that, I shall send for Lucy to hold your hands. You have shown the greatest courage and strength of character in this catastrophe. Do not behave like a child now. This document is of the greatest importance to you. Listen.'

The governess held the paper close to the candle. She read very slowly, pronouncing each word carefully and clearly.

' "This is to certify that on the 18th March 1772, I, Theodore Henry Wilkinson, minister of religion in the service of the Honourable East India Company in Madras, conducted a service of matrimony between Francis George Delaney, baronet, Captain of Artillery, and Zobeida, daughter of His Highness the Rajah of Benpore. The witnesses to this ceremony were Nathaniel Stimson, engineer, since deceased, and His Highness. Also present were my wife, Catherine, and my servant, Dasim Ali, a Mohammedan who had been baptised into the Christian church." '

IX

There were three things which had to be done, and from all of them Phyllida's thoughts shied away. She had to confront Francis with the proof of his marriage. She must receive her uncle's notary. Worst of all, there was a letter to be written to Edward Glenister. Yet that seemed to her the most important.

She sat for an hour at the desk in the parlour, and the charred remains of her efforts damped down the fire. She felt like a child again, set some task beyond her capabilities. This room, it occurred to her, had been the scene of almost everything unpleasant that had happened to her. Here, Lord Stansted had made that shaming examination of her person which now she understood. Here, her guardian had upbraided her two nights ago. Was it really as recently as that? And here, less than twenty-four hours ago, she had refused to listen to the man who had put himself out to help her, and accused him of planning murder, just as Uncle Samuel had done. She had been as grossly unjust to Edward as her guardian had been to herself.

What words could she use to excuse herself? There *was* no excuse, save that she had been utterly distraught, beaten down by a succession of shocks and by a call upon her strength and courage which, in the last resort, had been unavailing.

The house was shrouded in silence. No longer could she hear the cook's tuneless humming, the kitchen boy's peals of laughter or sudden yelp of pain as his ears were boxed. Straw had been laid on the stable yard so that not even the hooves of the horses being exercised made any clatter. All windows fronting the street had their shutters closely shut. In a room upstairs the seamstress and her assistant were hard at work making her a black gown, the first of several which for a year would replace the blues and greens and lemons which she favoured. As the news spread round the neighbourhood, cards were left, people called. Phyllida refused to see anybody, leaving Henty to receive visitors. It was too soon. She was too troubled, not only by her guardian's death, but by the manner of it, and all the misunderstandings which had thereby arisen.

At last she decided she could do no better. She sanded and sealed her letter and rang for Harry.

'You are to take this to Clavant Manor without delay. And, Harry, if Mr. Glenister is home, you are to wait for an answer.'

She was in her bedroom, trying on the finished gown, when Henty came to tell her that Francis Delaney was below, asking to be received. Phyllida was tempted to refuse him too. Yet what point was there in putting off this difficult meeting?

'Very well,' she said with as much determination as

she could command. 'You may inform him that I will be down directly.'

She kept him waiting while the final adjustments were made. She frowned into her mirror, hating the unrelieved black which seemed to take all colour, all vitality from her face.

'I would prefer to see him alone,' she told the governess, making ready to accompany her.

Inevitably, she thought, this meeting must take place in the parlour. For the drawing-room was shuttered, the door closed, and her uncle's body lay there in its coffin, awaiting this evening's burial. In any case, she believed it would be a long time before she could bring herself to enter that room again.

Francis was dressed in a grey suit with a flowered waistcoat. One hand rested negligently upon his sword hilt. He made her an elegant bow.

'Your servant, ma'am. It is indeed good of you to receive me.'

Her curtsey barely creased her skirt. Unhurriedly she sat down and studied his face. There was a puffiness about his eyes, and on his right cheek a weal showed where she had struck him with her whip. That incident seemed to her now a lifetime away, instead of only yesterday; and she herself a different, far older person.

He laid his arm along the back of her chair in a proprietary manner. 'I called, naturally, to offer my condolences, and what help I may. In our especial relationship, doubtless you would be more than grateful to leave all legal affairs in my hands. 'Tis not seemly for a woman to . . .'

'Captain Delaney,' she broke in coldly, 'I have agreed to receive you so soon after my guardian's death for one purpose only. To put an end to our—especial relationship, as you term it.'

He appeared only mildly surprised at her statement.

'Miss Marchant, I assure you there is not the slightest need for you to feel this is necessary. I am perfectly prepared to wait until your period of mourning is over.'

She stared at him, disconcerted by his bland manner.

'You misunderstand me, sir. There can be no question any longer of marriage, even betrothal, between us.'

He laughed affectedly and moved away from her chair. 'I quite realise, ma'am, that in your estimation I behaved somewhat indiscreetly the last time we were together. But, i' faith, you made me pay for it.' Lightly he touched his cheek. 'I shall not make such a mistake again, I promise you. You may rest assured that in your present unfortunate position I shall conduct myself with the utmost propriety.'

Her tone was icy. 'How you conduct yourself in future, sir, is no concern of mine. It is how you have behaved in the past which now stands between us.'

He glanced up from studying his finger-nails and for the first time appeared to notice the paper in her hand. The slightest frown showed on his handsome face.

'I am at a loss to understand you, ma'am.'

She thrust the document towards him. 'I have no doubt this will make matters plain.'

As he read, she studied him again with a detachment which surprised her. It seemed incredible that she had ever been afraid of him. She had been ignorant then, and in his power. Now he was in hers. Thanks to Edward Glenister, she reminded herself ruefully. An unfamiliar sense of triumph laid hold of her. For the first time in this room she felt herself to be in control.

She said bitingly, 'I trust you do not intend to deny the truth of that statement.'

He handed it back to her with a careless gesture. 'Naturally I shall not deny it. But I venture to suggest it cannot have the slightest bearing on the matter of our marriage.'

Taken aback, she blurted out, 'How can that be?'

'Because I am sure that Zobeida is no longer alive. Indian women, you see, have a touching custom. When they believe their husband to be dead, they set themselves alight upon a funeral pyre. They term it suttee. A pity, in Zobeida's case. She was very beautiful, even by European standards.'

Phyllida's calmness abruptly deserted her. She half rose, gripping the arms of her chair. 'How can you stand there and be so callous? Do you mean to say that you deliberately gave this poor girl to believe that you were dead? That you left India knowing what would happen to her? Why, such behaviour is tantamount to—to murder.'

His hand tightened on his sword. His eyes narrowed. 'I should take care, madam, how you use that word. After all, I was sober enough to realise what was intended last night. Glenister sent his servant to kill me, and I have no doubt you were party to that plan.'

She rose and faced him, hands clenched at her sides, her lower lip thrust out. 'Neither you nor Uncle Samuel had the slightest reason for making such an accusation.'

'So your guardian had the same idea? I vow I'd scarcely have credited it of either of you. In India Glenister was always so perfectly correct, never even casting a glance at another woman despite having to endure that whining misery of a wife. And you, so divinely innocent, so very properly shocked when I so much as dared to . . .'

'Captain Delaney.' Her voice was under tight control. 'I should be obliged if you would leave this house at once.'

He made no move, only regarded her with insolent amusement. 'You seem to forget, ma'am, that there is a contract of marriage between us. You are bound to me, whether the idea appeals to you or not. And, i' faith, the prospect of marrying you begins to intrigue me. 'Tis a long time since I have tamed a wayward woman. A pity it means a year of waiting to have you as my wife. But there's no reason why I should not have you in my bed before then.'

There was a heavy silver candlestick on the table beside her. Every impulse tempted her to pick it up and bring it crashing down on his head. Instead, she dug her nails into her palms, took a deep breath. She spoke each word separately and deliberately.

'Captain Delaney, if it meant that I die unwed, or ended my days in prison or the madhouse, I would rather any of those fates than be forced to marry you. I know now a little of what your mother suffered, why she chose death beneath the wheels of your father's carriage rather than continue the humiliation of her life. You may take what steps you wish regarding the contract made between your uncle and mine. You may even have whatever money I possess, if the lawyers so insist. But I do assure you, you will never have me.'

She turned and jerked at the bell rope. It was obvious that William had been waiting close at hand, for the door opened immediately.

Francis still stood his ground. His eyes ranged over her, from head to toe. Then he laughed.

'You're a fool, Phyllida Marchant. I'd have launched you into London society, made you . . .' He broke off, shrugging. 'There's no accounting for women. That girl in India could have had her pick of minor but wealthy princes. Instead, she set her heart upon me, an almost penniless junior officer. You, who could have all London at your feet, prefer to bury yourself in the country with a man who'll bore you to tears within a year, and a chit of a child, another woman's child. I wish you joy.'

As he bowed mockingly before her, she said coldly, 'You are as mistaken as my guardian was, sir. I have not the slightest intention of marrying Mr. Glenister, nor has there been more than a casual acquaintance between us. The man I wish to marry is someone quite, quite different.'

Half turned towards the door, he looked straight into her eyes. She read surprise, then doubt and finally incredulity in his expression.

At last he said, 'Can it be so? Then to what end is Glenister putting himself out on your behalf? And what game are you yourself playing?' Again he touched his cheek. 'A docile, innocent, sweet young girl. That is how they described you to me. I' faith, how blind can men be?' He shrugged and put on his gold-laced tricorne at a jaunty angle. 'It seems more sensible on my part to make my peace with my Uncle Stansted and prevail upon him to find me a more willing heiress. I bid you good-day, ma'am, and farewell.'

The door had scarcely closed behind him when it opened again to admit Harry. The groom's clothes were spattered with mud, his boots plastered with chalky earth.

'I got caught in a heavy shower over Clavant way, ma'am,' he explained. 'You know how the clouds mount up over the downs and sometimes we miss a storm here when they have it a few miles away, and sometimes 'tis the other way round.'

'Yes, yes,' she said impatiently. 'Have you brought me an answer from Mr. Glenister?'

He shook his head regretfully. 'No, Miss Phyllida, I'm sorry.'

She turned away, loath to let him see the depth of her disappointment. 'Mr. Glenister gave you no message at all, not even by a servant?'

'Well, he couldn't really, ma'am, seeing as how he wasn't at the manor.'

She swung round. 'Why did you not say so at once?'

'You didn't ask me, ma'am.'

She was about to voice her exasperation. Then, remembering his loyalty, his rescue of her yesterday, she asked instead, 'He is perhaps in Chichester?'

'No, Miss Phyllida, he's gone further afield than that.'

'What do you mean? Oh, Harry, tell me quickly.'

'The truth is, ma'am, I was informed by his housekeeper that Mr. Glenister set out this morning in his carriage—for London, seemingly.'

She gazed at him in disbelief. 'For *London?* In late November? The roads will be in a shocking state. And he scarcely recovered from the fever.'

The groom tilted up his wig to scratch his head. 'It does seem a mite strange now you come to think of it. But that's what the housekeeper said. He'd gone to London, and no notion of when he'd be returning. Course, begging your pardon, Miss Phyllida, we all know as Mr. Glenister's a gentleman what likes to keep his affairs to himself. When he was staying at the Dolphin and Anchor, he was never free with his talk like some as they've had putting up there.'

'You are right,' she agreed, and there was bitterness in her voice. 'And because of his reserve he lays himself open to being constantly misjudged. If he had not kept silent, time and again when I . . .' She broke off, suddenly aware of the curiosity in the groom's eyes. 'Thank you, Harry. You may go.'

At the door he turned. 'Am I to exercise Centaur for you, Miss Phyllida, seeing as how it's not fitting for you to ride out yet awhile?'

She was troubled by his question. It had seemed to her throughout this long day that life had virtually stopped. Yet of course it was not so. Despite the quiet which prevailed in the house, despite the closed door of the drawing-room, the routine of the house had continued without pause. Meals had been prepared, beds made, fires lit. And horses had to be cared for, whether the master was dead or alive.

'If you please,' she answered Harry. 'I suppose I cheated Uncle Samuel in a way. He ordered Centaur to be shot, you remember. It was, I think, the only time I ever really disobeyed him.'

After Harry had gone, she buried her face in her hands. With the death of her guardian, the world was a dark and frightening place again. She had no idea what would happen to her. It had been easy enough to make those rash statements to Francis, angry as she had been then. But to face the reality of perhaps being penniless, without a home, without any experience of working for her keep—that was a different matter. If the worst should happen, and her dowry be forfeited by her refusal to marry Francis, she supposed she could obtain a post as governess, to some family in the town. Why, there was a post already waiting, not twenty miles from Chichester. Emma Glenister was in need of a governess, and would be overjoyed to have her at the manor.

'I could be a governess,' she said aloud, 'at "Lady Sarah's house".' And burst out laughing.

Henty, coming into the room, hearing the nature of that laugh, slapped Phyllida hard across the cheek.

'That is enough, miss. I know full well you are distressed by all that has happened. But you will continue to exercise the self-control I have always taught you. I will not tolerate hysteria.'

It was after the notary had called on her that Phyllida first noticed the changed attitude of the staff at Meadhayes. No longer did they treat her with the tolerant indulgence accorded her since childhood. The women's curtsies now were markedly deferential, the menservants' bows very correct. Even Henty, looking drawn and haggard, adopted a gentler tone and was rarely censorious. Only Lucy had not changed, and it was she who enlightened Phyllida.

' 'Tis like this, ma'am. You're the mistress now. We all know that you're Mr. Gunter's sole beneficiary, him having quarrelled with all the rest of his family and that not surprising to my way o' thinking.'

'How do you know this? Not one of you, not even Miss Henty, was present when I received my uncle's lawyer.'

Lucy's answer was carefully casual. 'We get news below stairs one way and another, 'tis best I keep silent as to how. You could dismiss us today if you'd a mind to. You've but the notary to answer to and he'll not argue with you on account of the fat fees he'll expect for looking after your affairs. Why, Miss Phyllida, you're a wealthy young lady now seemingly, and there's none so glad as myself. Once you're out of mourning, you can be free as air, like you've always wanted.'

She found it impossible to believe. She had expected to find there was some document which denied her a penny if she did not conform to her guardian's wishes in the matter of her marriage. There was none. The lawyer had explained, choosing his words carefully, that he understood the contract was a verbal one between Mr. Gunter and Lord Stansted, that the matter had involved certain delicate transactions which were best not committed to paper. She had accepted his explanation without questioning him further, only too relieved to find she was free of Francis Delaney for good. When she discovered she was to inherit Uncle Samuel's fortune she had felt a certain sense of guilt, since he had died suspecting her of a terrible crime. Had she the right to accept his money in those circumstances? Yet in her heart she knew herself innocent. And she had never, except for the matter of refusing to have her horse shot, given him anything but obedience and loyalty, however unwilling she had been to accept the future he had planned for her.

The idea of having power over other people, of being free to make more than minor decisions for the first time in her life, was at first a little frightening. She called the servants together and assured them she had no intention of making any changes. She asked for their support in this difficult time and gave them all an immediate rise in wages. It was impossible to think beyond the present, beyond this seemingly endless succession of days, confined to the house by the rigid etiquette of mourning.

At the end of a week she began to receive callers, matching her manner to the austerity of her dress. But beneath her outward calm she was immensely troubled. In the night she would wake trembling, hearing again her guardian's voice uttering that dreadful accusation at the very time she was striving to save his life. In the enclosed darkness she would hear another voice, her own, blazing out those unjust suspicions against Edward Glenister, blaming him just as unfairly as she had been blamed by Uncle Samuel.

If only he had not gone away before her letter of apology, with its desperate plea for forgiveness, could reach him. Not, she reflected bitterly, that it would be of any importance to him that she knew him innocent of anything save a desire to help her. For had he not told her that other people's opinions mattered little to him now? But *his* opinion of *her*, she discovered, to her dismay, mattered a great deal.

She missed his presence. She missed Emma dreadfully. She longed for Kit. Always in the past she had poured out all her troubles to him and he had listened patiently, given her good advice or laughed away her fears. She would have welcomed one of his 'lectures' if only she could have had him near her at this time.

At the end of ten days she would even have welcomed one of the hitherto tedious tea-parties Henty had insisted she attend. She wandered from room to room, finding trivial, unnecessary tasks to occupy her brain and fingers.

More than anything she desired a gallop over the downs to release her pent-up energy, to free her mind of its turbulent thoughts. On a day at the end of November which seemed borrowed from spring, she could stand the enforced confinement within doors no longer. To her surprise, when she announced her intention of riding out, saying she would take Harry with her, the governess made no protest.

'You are indeed looking pale, child,' Miss Henty said sympathetically. 'It will do you good to have some fresh air. But, Phyllida, take care. You have not ridden that wild chestnut for two weeks.'

Phyllida rode circumspectly along North Street, feeling strange in a black habit instead of her favourite green. She looked straight ahead, ignoring the covert glances, the murmurs which greeted her appearance. Past the alms houses and up on to the track to the downs she curbed Centaur's impatience and her own. The track led to the derelict cottage which was one of her former meeting-places with Kit. It struck her for the first time that when Kit returned from London, there would be nothing to prevent her meeting him quite openly. With Uncle Samuel's death, all need for secrecy was over. Everything now was changed. Her freedom was too new, too unfamiliar to accept yet. Her freedom, and all its implications.

She dismissed Harry, gave the chestnut its head. He sprang forward and galloped up the track, then swung away left over the short turf of the downs, scattering the sheep. The blue sky was cloudless, the air crisp. In the distance the sea glittered, the cathedral tower soared above the rooftops, a landmark for miles around.

Caught by the breeze at the top of the hill, the chestnut's mane and tail streamed out; he tossed his head in sheer exhilaration. Phyllida's cheeks tingled, her body rejoiced in attuning itself to the rhythm of the horse's action. Her mind became emptied of everything save its joyful awareness of the beauty of sky and sunlight and the green grass beneath Centaur's pounding hooves.

She drew rein at last, laughing and breathless, and looked about her. She had lost all sense of direction in this wild, headlong gallop in which she had given Centaur his head, content to let him take her where he would. She was on a hill above Clavant, on the opposite side of the valley to her usual route there. Quite clearly she could see 'Lady Sarah's house'. Smoke curled from its chimneys, a maid shook a duster from an upstairs window; a groom walked a horse in the yard. In the clear air she could hear a dog barking. All this she had imagined as a child: the empty house coming to life, being lived in, being loved. And herself its mistress.

She walked the chestnut along the ridge of the hill and let her gaze wander slowly over every inch of the house and garden. There was the drawing-room window through which she had so often peered, weaving her fantasies. There was the fountain, pouring water into its ornamental basin; the rose-beds which had been choked with weeds. There was the rebuilt length of wall where once had been the gap through which she and Kit had scrambled. She saw herself, three years ago, following Kit towards their horses, heard herself saying, 'How wonderful it would be if you were Sir Francis Delaney and we could be married and live here happily for ever and ever.'

Her mind cleared by the fresh, strong air, and exercise, she faced the full implication of her new freedom. She could marry Kit. A year of mourning, a request to the notary who, Lucy had assured her, would accede to her every wish, and her dearest dream would come true. One of her dreams, she corrected herself. For they would not live in 'Lady Sarah's house'.

But might not even that be possible? Had not Francis been sure he could buy the house for her, with her dowry?

'Glenister is a merchant,' he had said, 'trained always to seek a profit.'

What if she should offer him a generous figure? Would he accept? Then she would have Kit, *and* 'Lady Sarah's house'. All her dreams would come true.

She wondered why she did not feel elated, thrilled at the prospect. But then, it would be wrong to feel joyous at this time. Her clothes betokened her mourning. Her thoughts should be in tune with them. If her dreams came true, it would be entirely due to Uncle Samuel's death. They would be purchased with his money.

Would Edward Glenister sell? It was not true that he always sought a profit. Had he not generously paid for Kit to go to London to study there? Had he not done his best to prevent her marriage to Francis, with no advantage to himself? Had he not, on each occasion she had met him, shown her the utmost kindness despite her constant misjudgment of him, the wicked accusations she had made against him? But would he continue to do so, after her last, terrible injustice towards him?

From this vantage point she could see all the activities of the manor. She saw the front door open and Emma run out, dressed in a scarlet cloak and bonnet; then turn and wait for somebody behind her. Then Edward himself, tall, erect, his fair hair shining in the sunlight.

So he was back. And he had not sent her a word. Her throat contracted. The downs, the colourful November woods, blurred before her eyes. She had done her best to atone, she had thrown herself upon his mercy. And he had met her plea with silence, with a cold disregard of which she had not thought him capable. She would rather by far have endured anger, scorn, even the superior attitude which had so irked her. Anything, rather than this ignoring of her letter, which meant he cared not one jot in what light she regarded him. More than anything that had happened to her in the past weeks, that thought seemed the greatest hurt of all.

The chestnut pricked his ears, jerked up his head. Phyllida heard the thud of hooves to her right. Someone was riding through the wood, upon the path which would join the track ahead of her. Between the trunks of the trees she saw a flurry of leaves, caught a momentary glimpse of the horseman. She caught her breath. She must be dreaming. Then, as he crossed an open glade, she saw him clearly. Brown suit, brown hair untidily escaping from its ribbon, a plain black tricorne; the sturdy brown cob.

'Kit.'

She whispered the name doubtfully, then said it again aloud, with certainty. She touched Centaur with her whip. As he sprang forward she saw the dear, familiar figure emerge from the wood.

'Kit! Kit, wait for me!'

He turned in the saddle, reined in and swung the cob round on its haunches.

'Phyllida! What are you doing up here?'

With difficulty she controlled Centaur and said breathlessly, 'I should ask *you* that question.'

'That is easily answered. I have just been setting Farmer Hardham's arm. He fell in the barn and . . .'

'But I thought you to be in London. Why have you returned? And—oh, Kit, you did not even let me know.'

'I arrived home only yesterday evening. I called at Meadhayes this morning and was told you had gone riding, no one knew where. While I was there, a servant came with news of Farmer Hardham's accident, and, my father being already called out in the opposite direction, I attended.'

'That does not explain why you left London,' she

pointed out, her voice light with happiness at seeing him.

'Oh, that. The fact is, Mr. Glenister came to fetch me.'

She stared at him incredulously. 'What did you say?'

'He drove up in his own carriage, and explained the position to the authorities at the hospital . . .'

'What position, Kit? What has happened to occasion you to leave the hospital?'

'Not to leave it, Phyllida. Only to absent myself for a few days, a week, perhaps.'

'But why, Kit? Why?'

He frowned with impatience. 'Because of what has happened to you, of course. He said you were distressed, which was natural considering the circumstances, and that my presence might be of benefit to you.'

For a few moments she could not speak. At last she asked, 'Do you mean to tell me that Mr. Glenister drove up to London, at this time of year, and scarcely recovered from fever, to fetch you back—for my sake?'

'Yes, that *is* what I mean.'

She urged Centaur forward so that he should not see her face. Tears were in her eyes again, she did not clearly know their cause. She had never felt so ashamed in her life. That this man who barely ten minutes ago she had thought uncaring, turning his back upon her at last, should have done this for her . . . And why? What had she ever done for him save try to help him when he had the fever, and bring some happiness to his motherless daughter, which in its turn had given *her* pleasure?

Kit drew level with her. 'It was a dreadful journey, Phyllida, and the inns where we put up were so dirty. The carriage broke down three times, and two horses went lame. We had to walk for quite a distance on two occasions. But that gave me the chance to attend to a sick woman in a cottage where we sought shelter.' His voice took on an eager note. 'I have learned so much in

London. It is all so interesting and exciting. I count myself most fortunate to be with such skilled men as are at the hospital.'

She could not follow what he was saying. It was connected with some marvellous new medical discovery, she gathered. After a few moments she ceased even to listen to his words, hearing only his voice, the voice which in the past had been the dearest in the world to her. She studied him as he rode beside her. The buttons of the brown suit were strained, his breeches were stretched tightly over his bulging calves. His face was fatter, his eyes bright and shining. London, it seemed, agreed with Kit in every way.

He patted his saddlebags. 'I have my own leeches now, and a bleeding cup and a few instruments.'

She could not stop herself saying, 'Bought for you by Mr. Glenister?'

Kit flushed and answered brusquely. 'I am not beholden to him for everything.'

'But I am.'

Kit, unaware of the humiliation behind her words, said in a self-satisfied tone, 'I told you, Phyllida, that he would be the one to help you. You would not believe me.'

She bent her head, twisting the long strands of Centaur's mane between her gloved fingers. 'I had to find out for myself. I have wronged him time and time again. I even accused him of murder.'

'*Phyllida!*'

'Did he not tell you that, during your long journey?'

Kit shook his head. 'He told me you were very distraught and greatly in need of comfort.'

'Which I am.' She said the words so softly he did not hear them.

His tone was censorious. 'Phyllida, will you never learn? I have told you often enough that you speak and act upon impulse, without giving time for considered judgment.'

'You are right, of course,' she agreed wearily. 'You always are. Mr. Glenister once said that his learning was gained in the hardest school of all, experience. It seems that is the way it has happened with me of late.'

Frowning, Kit said, 'I only hope that by your latest folly you have not prejudiced my chances.'

'*Your* chances? How can my behaviour affect your career?'

He bent down, fidgeting with a stirrup leather that appeared perfectly in order to her.

'Kit,' she insisted, 'how are your medical studies bound up with how I conduct myself towards Mr. Glenister? Ah, I remember now, that last time we met, you were so secretive. You suggested that Mr. Glenister would make things come right for us both, and I did not understand your meaning. I still do not.'

Kit straightened. 'Let us canter a little. It grows cold just walking the horses.'

She sighed. 'You are right again. Centaur will get chilled after his hard gallop.'

They rode down the track side by side as of old. But she felt uneasy. There was something to be said which Kit found difficult, and she was sure it would not be to her liking. She waited, curbing her impatience, until he should find the right words.

At last he slowed the cob to a trot and cleared his throat. 'The fact is, Phyllida, that Mr. Glenister is not paying for my training entirely for my sake.'

'For whose, then?'

'Yours.'

'How can that be?'

'I understand you have more than once expressed to him your desire to marry me. There were three obstacles to that. Your uncle, Francis Delaney, and my lack of means. Mr. Glenister, directly or indirectly, has removed the first two. The third he was prepared to overcome also, by sending me to London.'

She rode in silence, trying to take in what he had said. At last she asked, 'Why should he concern himself so much in our affairs? We are comparative strangers to him.'

'*Your* affairs, Phyllida,' he corrected. 'I realise now that his interest in me is because he regards me as the man you wish to marry.'

'I still do not see why. After all, I have done nothing to deserve such kindness. In fact, at times I have given him every cause to hate me.'

Kit shrugged. 'He has told me a little about his marriage. It seems he is never without a sense of guilt for the sickness and unhappiness his wife suffered in India. Though I cannot see why. It is obvious from his conversation that he told her all the facts about what she must face in that country before ever she left England. My guess is that she was a plain woman without a dowry, with little chance of marriage here and so leaped at his offer. And then never ceased to complain when she found conditions in Madras no better than he had described them.'

'And so he is helping us—me, if you insist, as a form of atonement?' It seemed an unlikely idea to her, and a bleak one.

'I can offer no other explanation. The most obvious reason why a man puts himself out so greatly for a woman, because he is in love with her, surely cannot apply. For if it did, he would set out to win you for himself, not be so eager to thrust you into my arms.'

'Of course he is not in love with me.'

As she uttered the denial, deep inside her there was a pain as sharp as a sword thrust. Yet still she did not understand. She only knew that her emotions were out of control, as disconcerting as they had been when she could not resist the temptation to put her arm around Edward's shoulders.

She said thoughtfully, 'So Mr. Glenister has given you a—a kind of ultimatum? That he pays for your training on the understanding that at the end of it you marry me.'

'That is so.' There was little enthusiasm in Kit's voice, she noticed. 'And then I believe he intends to make over to us the manor house at Clavant.'

'*What?*'

She reined in, completely taken aback. 'Kit, do you know what you are saying?'

Reluctantly he halted beside her. 'Of course. I do not make wild statements without foundation, as you are well aware. He has not said this in so many words. But he made it plain enough. It is, I fully believe, why he furnished the drawing-room to your taste.'

Again she rode ahead so that he should not see her face. She thought she had already reached the depths of shame and humiliation. But this further evidence of Edward's consideration and generosity towards her was almost beyond bearing.

Angrily she brushed the tears from her eyes. She spoke without turning her head. 'Kit, you cannot accept this. *I* cannot accept it. Not after the way I have treated him.'

He caught up with her but seemed unaware of her distress. 'You are in a position now to buy the house from him if you still want it so very much.'

She kept her face averted while she asked, with sudden insight, 'You would not want to live there, would you, Kit?'

'Well, as to that, you know that the place has never had the same attraction for me. A little town house would do well enough for my needs.'

'In Chichester? Or in London?' She turned to study his reaction.

His face reddened. He said awkwardly, 'There is of course more scope in London.'

She rode for a while in silence. She had thought herself free to order her life as she wished. But she was not. The two objects of her dreams, marriage to Kit and the possession of 'Lady Sarah's house' were now within reach. But instead of being able to stretch out her hand to take them, they were being thrust at her, almost forced upon her. She was being tied to her dreams now by Edward Glenister's generosity. And she knew, with a sudden sensation of chill and emptiness throughout her body, that she did not want to be tied to them. While they *were* only dreams, part of a nebulous future, they caused her no misgivings. Now, faced with their coming true, she was afraid and strangely reluctant.

Into her mind's eye came again that picture of herself gazing into the drawing-room of the empty manor house, seeing its furnishings in imagination, hearing music, never able to put faces to the shadowy figures who had peopled the room for her. Now, before her eyes, there were faces. Her own, Henty's, Emma's. But not Kit's. Instead, she saw in every detail, as she had done that day in the drawing-room at Meadhayes, Edward's face. And at last she understood.

She exclaimed aloud, and shivered involuntarily.

'We had best hurry,' Kit said. 'I told you it was growing chill.'

When they reached Meadhayes, for the first time he followed her openly into the stable yard.

'You will stay to dinner?' she asked, trying to force warmth into her voice.

Helping her to dismount, he shook his head. 'Thank you, but I think not. My father is very overworked. He will be grateful if I help him with his medicines and accounts.'

It was suddenly borne in on Phyllida that not once since they met had he offered her a word of comfort or expressed regret for what had happened. He had not even asked in what way he could help her, even though Edward had fetched him back from London for that express purpose.

As he turned away she caught at his arm. 'Kit, before you go, I pray you answer me one question.'

He frowned but waited, the cob's reins looped over his arm, while she looked at him, long and searchingly.

She said at last, 'It is this. Do you wish to marry me?'

He took a step backward. The colour flooded up from his neck into his cheeks. He bit his lip. 'Phyllida, it has always been understood between us that if it were possible . . .'

'I did not ask you that. You are a great stickler for the truth, Kit. I pray you speak it now.'

He could not meet her eyes. He wound the rein uselessly round and round his wrist. His voice was muffled, unfamiliar.

'I—I have no wish to hurt you, Phyllida . . .'

'You will not,' she assured him, and knew with astonished relief that it was true. 'What has hurt me is the lies I have been told, the ignorance in which I have been kept, the knowledge that those I thought good were not so, that the one I tried to hate has proved himself to be . . . You do not wish to marry me after all, do you, Kit?'

He raised troubled eyes. There was distress in every line of his face. 'I—I am not sure. The fact is that I am at present so absorbed in medicine that any thought of marriage, or even betrothal, is difficult to contemplate. Phyllida, I am truly sorry to answer you in this fashion. I am very fond of you. I always have been, as you must know. But as to marrying you . . .'

Somewhere above her head a window was closed. The clang of metal came from the stables. A cart passed along the street, the sheep in it bleating noisily. Familiar sounds, as those sounds she had heard at her last meeting with Kit beside the derelict cottage had been familiar. On that occasion she had been full of sorrow, knowing Kit was leaving her, aware that in thought he had already gone a long way from her. Now, there was only this surprising sense of relief. She had thought to be faced with yet another conflict. And it had been resolved for her by Kit himself.

She said slowly, 'Once, if you had spoken those words to me, I should have believed my heart to be broken. Now, I can accept them with no more than a passing regret. I think our love—our affection—was a childish affair, Kit. You have entered into a new life which offers you all you want at present. And I—I have grown up, Kit. I do not really know what I want, not yet. But I will not have you tied, as I was tied. You must allow me to pay for the remainder of your training, and there will be no strings attached. No, do not argue,' she exclaimed as she saw the stubborn set of his mouth. 'It will please me to do this for you, as a return for all you have taught me, all the happiness you gave me when I was lonely. Please, Kit, let me have my way in this.'

'Phyllida.' He took hold of her hands and helplessly shook his head. 'I am sorry,' he said again.

She smiled at him. 'You have no need to be.' She managed to force a little gaiety into her voice. 'Have I not said often enough that we should not really suit?'

He bent forward and kissed her cheek. 'You begged me so often to tell you that I loved you, and I did because it pleased you so. I think I was never more truthful in saying it than now, Phyllida. But it is not a love, I know now, upon which marriage should be based.'

'I know that too, Kit, now. I am no longer as ignorant of what marriage means. But I pray you, stay my friend.'

'Of course. I will come again tomorrow. If it is fine we could ride on the downs, race our horses as we used to do.'

She said with genuine warmth, 'I will look forward to that.'

He went from her then. She watched him ride out of the yard as Harry came to lead Centaur to the stables. She walked slowly towards the house, trying to resolve her feelings, trying to understand how her dreams could have been shattered, not by someone else, but by her own truant heart.

Lucy met her at the side door. The maid's cheeks were flushed, her eyes bright. She thrust a letter into Phyllida's hand.

'Mr. Glenister's groom came with this soon after you set out. I could scarce wait until Mr. Burrell had gone to give it you.'

With shaking fingers Phyllida broke the seal, unfolded the sheet of paper.

My dear Miss Phyllida, she read. *I surmise that by now Kit Burrell will have called upon you. That, I trust, will give you my answer to the letter which I fear must have caused you no little distress to write. Rest assured that I have erased the accusations you made, while under the greatest stress and grief, entirely from my memory. I pray you to do likewise. Think only of the future, when happiness may well be within your reach at last. When Kit has returned to London, I shall beg leave to call upon you, or to hope that you will come and see us at the manor. Emma has been in poor spirits during my absence and misses you greatly. As for myself, I am not at present the most cheerful of company for her, being saddened by the news I received in London. It seems*

*that Lord Clive, overburdened with pain and the wrongs
done to him, took his own life on the 22nd of this month.*
   I remain, dear Miss Phyllida,
                 Your most devoted servant,
                       Edward Glenister.

She read it through again and again until the words blurred before her eyes. Lucy stood silently by, twisting her apron between her fingers. At last she could restrain herself no longer.

'You're crying, ma'am. That means then, that Mr. Glenister . . .'

She looked up, smiling through her tears. 'It means he has forgiven me. Lucy, he has forgiven me entirely. And he—he wants to see me again.' She caught the maid's hands in her own. 'Did you hear, Lucy? He wants to see me again.'

Then, to the maid's utter astonishment, Phyllida danced her round the hall. Until, breathless, she fetched up opposite the closed door of the drawing-room. Abruptly she released Lucy's hands and raised her own to her flushed cheeks.

'Oh, how wicked I am! To be dancing, and Uncle Samuel scarce two weeks in his grave. Whatever will become of me?'

The maid, leaning puffing against the wall, chuckled. 'I could hazard a guess, ma'am. But 'tis best I keep silent and leave you to find out for yourself.'

X

As soon as she woke, Phyllida was aware of the gale. The window shutters rattled, the wind whined down the chimney. Even the bed curtains moved in the draughts circulating round her bedroom.

She pulled them back and rang for Lucy.

'Is it raining?' she asked when the maid appeared.

'No, ma'am. But blowing fit to lift the roof off. There'll be a fair sea running down on the coast. 'Tis a day when it's best not to venture out.'

Phyllida sipped her hot chocolate. 'Nevertheless, I shall go out.'

Lucy, in the act of opening the shutters, asked over her shoulder, 'You're not aiming to go far, surely? 'Tis a real first of December day. The rain will come later, I'll wager.'

'Then I had best take the carriage.' She explained with studied casualness, 'I intend visiting Mr. Glenister. It seems that Emma would be glad of my company.'

'And Mr. Glenister would not find it unwelcome, to my way o' thinking.'

Phyllida said primly, 'I shall sympathise with him in the matter of Lord Clive's death. I am sure the news will greatly have distressed him.'

'Yes, ma'am,' Lucy agreed demurely, but her eyes were dancing. 'And what shall I put out for you to wear?'

Phyllida sighed. 'I think the black gown the seamstress finished yesterday. It is at least a little more becoming than the ones she ran up so quickly two weeks ago.'

The maid held the gown at arms' length. ''Tis such a pity we can't have some soft white flounces at elbow and neck, ma'am. You do not look your best in black. But there, we'll put a little rouge on your cheeks and pile up your hair. And if you remember to bite your lips hard when you reach the manor, Mr. Glenister will think you as pretty as ever, for 'tis the best way I know to put colour into them. Will you be taking Miss Henty with you?'

Phyllida hesitated. 'Yes, I think I had better do so. It would be more seemly.'

She had, however, every intention of devising some pretext of getting rid of the governess when they arrived. This meeting with Edward was like to prove embarrassing enough without Henty being present. For how was she to convey to him her gratitude for all he had done to try to ensure her happiness, and at the same time reveal to him that her happiness was no longer linked with Kit? Would he think her fickle, an ingrate, disloyal and altogether weak and childish?

The wind stirred up the dust, sent the leaves dancing, and roared through the bare branches in the wood. The horses' manes were ruffled, their tails streamed out. Samuel and William held on to their hats. Miss Henty huddled into a corner of the carriage, a rug pulled tightly around her. She had pleaded one of her headaches. But, contrary to past practice, Phyllida had begged her to come. The governess, sighing, had agreed.

Phyllida glanced at the sky. Lucy had been right. There would be rain later. It had indeed been more sensible to come in the carriage. If, that was, it had been sensible to come at all.

At the top of the rise which gave a view of the valley, she looked out of the window. The vehicle was rocked from side to side by the force of the wind on the upland. Rooks were playing about the elms, tossed and tumbled in the turbulent air. Down in the village a child chased its hat across the green. In the grounds of the manor a man was tending a bonfire. The flames reared high. Smoke drifted across the side of the house. Phyllida thought it foolish that anyone should risk such a blaze in this gale. Even as she watched, a flurry of sparks flew upwards and landed on the roof of an outhouse—a thatched roof. In a moment it was ablaze.

Before her horrified eyes the flames swept on, under the fierce pressure of the wind. They licked at the stone walls, the windows of the manor house, seeking easy entry.

Phyllida flung down the window, shouted to Samuel, 'Whip up the horses! Make haste! Oh, make haste!'

Miss Henty fell against the opposite seat as the vehicle lurched forward. 'Whatever is the matter?' she gasped.

'It is "Lady Sarah's house",' Phyllida answered over her shoulder. 'It is catching fire. Oh, Hen, what *can* we do?'

It seemed an eternity before they reached the gates. Samuel could get the horses no further. They plunged and reared, all but upsetting the carriage. Phyllida wrenched open the door. Not even waiting for William to lower the steps, she bunched up her cloak and jumped to the ground. She ran wildly up the drive, with no real notion of what she intended. She knew only that she must get to the house. She must find Edward. And Emma.

Smoke blew into her face, making her gasp, her eyes smart. She heard the crash of timber, the crack of splintering glass. A terrified horse galloped headlong towards her. She flung herself aside just in time to avoid being run down. Above the noise of the fire she could hear the shrill whinnying of others still in the stables; shouts, women's screams, the frenzied barking of dogs.

Suddenly, she was in the midst of her old nightmare. Her legs lost their strength. She sank down on the edge of the stone basin of the fountain, put her hands over her ears. Fire. Fire, which had robbed her of her parents; out of which she had been plucked by brown hands, only to be held by the heels while a knife flashed towards her throat. It was here again, all around her, that terror of thirteen years ago. She knew she could not go on; that in a moment when her legs would support her, she would turn tail and flee, back to the safety of the carriage. To Samuel and William and Henty who would protect her from all danger.

She stood up, took her hands from her ears. It was then she heard the scream, higher pitched than the others. A child's scream, unmistakably. She turned towards the house, listening. Not wanting to listen. It came again, thinly, from one of the upper windows. Emma's voice. It must be.

Phyllida forced herself forward, peered upwards through the smoke. As it cleared momentarily, blown by the wind, she saw Emma's face, white, terrified, at the nursery window. And Emma was herself, all those years ago, crying out in a world of fear and blackness, and swift devouring flames. And no-one answering.

She clasped her cloak tightly about her, kilted up her skirt and ran forward. To her relief, she found the front door ajar. She sped across the hall and up the stairs. Inside the house, the fire sounded like the wind, a rising, falling roar. But for the moment the stairs were clear. She raced up the first flight, then the second, and flung open the nursery door. The room was full of smoke.

'Emma,' she gasped. 'Darling, where are you? Come to me. Here, by the door.'

In a moment the child was clinging to her, coughing and sobbing.

'Quickly. Take my hand.'

Phyllida ran swiftly down the upper stairs, pulling Emma with her. She started down the main staircase, then drew back, uttering a cry of dismay. The hall was ablaze. To reach the front door she would have to cross a very sea of flame.

She hesitated, looking wildly about her. Which way? Desperately she tried to remember the lay-out of the house she thought she knew so well. But her brain refused to answer her need.

A door crashed open behind her. Edward's voice called

urgently, 'This way. Come.'

Smoke blinded her. She could not see him. Her breath came in choking gasps. Emma clung to her, whimpering.

Then, hazily, she saw Edward beside them. He lifted Emma into his arms, caught Phyllida's hand and dragged her after him along a passage. She remembered now, of course. The back stairs.

She stumbled down them, through another narrow passage. Then, mercifully, she was outside the house. She leaned against the wall, taking great gulps of the blessed, smoke-free air.

Edward's voice was urgent. 'We must get further away from the house. There is danger of the roof collapsing.'

She staggered along behind him, clinging to his hand, gasping for breath. Through the roar and crackle of the fire she could hear men shouting. But now there were no women's screams, nor whinnying from the horses. She prayed it meant the servants were safe, the animals freed from the burning stables. At last through the smoke she saw ahead of them a rustic seat sheltered by a thick yew hedge. It was up-wind of the fire.

Thankfully she sank down and put a hand to her throat which felt quite raw. She coughed uncontrollably. Tears streamed down her face. Emma was in the same state as she clung to her father's neck.

Edward asked anxiously, 'You are unhurt?'

She dashed a hand across her smarting eyes. 'Completely. And Emma. She is but frightened, I think.'

'Thanks to you.' His voice was deep and husky. 'You risked your life, Phyllida. You might have been . . .'

'There was no other course. Emma called. I had to go.'

It seemed incredibly natural, not calling for any special courage. But now that it was over, she began to tremble.

He said, talking quickly, 'I was on the other side of

the river, inspecting some irrigation ditches. My horse took fright at the smell of fire and broke loose. I could not catch him. I had to walk, that was why I was so long. I thought—Emma, was ayah with you?'

The little girl shook her head.

'Where was she?' he asked gently. 'Try to tell me.'

The child's voice was muffled by sobs. 'She went to the kitchen, for my bread and milk.'

'Thank God for that!' he exclaimed. 'There is a chance then . . .' He glanced over his shoulder, his forehead creased with anxiety.

Phyllida sat up straight. 'Mr. Glenister, give Emma to me. I will look after her while you make sure everyone is out of the house.'

He looked relieved, then the anxiety returned to his face. 'I cannot leave you here.'

'Why not? We shall be safe enough. Your servants will be looking to you for orders.'

Still he hesitated. 'If you are sure . . .'

'I am quite sure,' she said steadily. She stretched out her arms. 'Come, darling. I will keep you warm inside my cloak.'

Gratefully he handed the child to her, then thrust a hand into his pocket. 'My flask,' he said, and smiled. 'You know by now, I think, its efficacy.'

With astonishment she heard herself laugh. The laugh was not very convincing. She hoped he did not notice the tremor.

'I shall become quite tipsy on your brandy, sir,' she said lightly.

'It will steady you.'

'I do not need steadying.' She thrust out a hand. 'See. I am not even—I am scarcely even trembling.'

Swiftly he bent and pressed her hand to his lips. His voice was as unsteady as her laugh had been. 'If you had been killed . . . Or Emma.'

She felt again as she had done that day at Meadhayes when he had the fever. Older than he, wanting to comfort. Lightly she pressed his fingers.

'But we were not,' she said calmly. 'It seems I am not to die by fire. It is the second time I have come through unscathed. Go now, you will be needed.'

Reluctantly he released her hand. 'I will be back as soon as I have made sure that everyone is safe.'

'My carriage is outside the gates. If I can, I will make my way towards it, with Emma. There are rugs inside to keep her warm. And then, with your permission, I will take her back to Meadhayes.'

'Thank you. That would be kind. If I do not see you . . .'

'I shall wait until you come.' Then, because of the way he was looking at her, she added impulsively, 'And, Edward, take care.'

He had the appearance of a man who had not clearly heard what was said to him.

He answered dazedly, 'Of course. I will come to you, beyond the gates.' Then abruptly he turned and strode quickly off.

Phyllida watched until his tall figure was lost in the billowing smoke. Then she unscrewed the familiar silver flask and poured a little brandy into the top.

'Drink this, very, very slowly,' she said, holding it to Emma's lips.

The child sipped, and spluttered, but drank all that was poured out. She shivered.

'Ugh! It is horrible. What will it do to me?'

'Make you warm inside.'

Emma snuggled up against Phyllida inside the folds of her thick cloak. 'That will be nice. I am very cold.' She looked up into Phyllida's face. 'Will you really take me home with you? And may I sleep in your bedroom, in case I am frightened? Though I do not think I shall be now that that horrid man is not there.'

'Emma, you must not . . .'

'Why must I not? He *was* horrid. That was why Dasim Ali killed him. Though he did not mean to kill your uncle. He meant to kill the other man, the one who would have made you so unhappy.'

'Darling, how do you know all this?'

The little girl nodded wisely. 'I heard Dasim Ali and ayah talking. Sometimes they forgot I understand Hindustani. It made Papa very unhappy. Did it make you unhappy, Miss Phyllida? Is that why you did not come to see us? Is that why you are dressed all in black?'

'Emma, you are not old enough to worry your head about such matters. And, as usual, you ask too many questions. See, I am going to drink some brandy now. You may hold the flask.'

Afterwards, Phyllida laid the flask on the seat beside her. As she did so, she caught sight of something glittering on the ground at her feet. Curious, she bent and picked it up.

Uncomprehendingly at first she stared at what lay in her palm. Her mind went back to a hot summer's day, up on the downs, the day Edward had rescued her after Centaur had thrown her and bolted. She was sitting on a grass bank while he wiped the dirt from her face, so gently, so very gently. She was bidding him leave her as they neared the city wall, holding out her hand in farewell. And as she did so, noticing the loss of a button from the sleeve of her light green riding suit. The button that lay now in her palm, polished and shining.

As if from a long way off, she heard Emma's voice.

'That is Papa's. He must have pulled it from his pocket with his brandy flask, and dropped it.'

With difficulty Phyllida brought her mind back to the present. 'You have seen it before?'

'Oh, yes. I think it is a sort of lucky charm. Papa often

takes it out and looks at it. He would have been very sorry if you had not found it.'

Phyllida closed her fingers around the button. 'Then I will keep it safe, and give it back to him, when the opportunity occurs.'

Emma stared up at her. 'Miss Phyllida, you are smiling. How can you look so happy when our house is burning down?'

What had Kit said, that day when she had learned that 'Lady Sarah's house' was not to be hers after all? 'Women should break their hearts over men, not over houses.' It was true, as most things Kit said were true. But she had had to find it out for herself.

She held the little girl close and laid her cheek against the fair ringlets. She spoke very softly.

'Houses are but bricks and wood and glass, Emma. They can be built up again. It is the people inside them who matter.'

'Yes, I see,' said Emma doubtfully. 'Will Papa build another house, then? And now that your uncle is dead, could you not come and live in it with us? I should like that very much, and so would papa.'

'And so would I,' Phyllida said, but only to herself.

The rain Lucy had prophesied came suddenly upon them, blowing in gusts across the valley. Phyllida made her way to the gates, skirting the outbuildings, the smoke. She caught glimpses of figures running to and fro. She could hear the clatter of buckets, and faintly, Edward's voice, giving orders.

Samuel was standing at the horses' heads in the shelter of the high wall. William was supporting Miss Henty who looked deathly pale.

She stumbled forward. 'Phyllida, where *have* you been? I sent William after you, but nobody had seen you at all. My dear child . . .'

Phyllida put an arm around the governess' shoulders.

'It is all right, Hen. I am unharmed. See, I have brought Emma. Get back into the carriage, you will become chilled standing here.'

Without a word Henty obeyed her. Phyllida settled Emma in a cocoon of rugs and left her in the governess' charge.

'Be gentle with her, Hen. She has had a great fright.'

As she descended the carriage steps she heard Emma's voice, clear and confident. 'Indeed, I was very frightened. I was in the nursery all alone and there was a lot of smoke and I called and called and nobody answered. And then Miss Phyllida came and rescued me. Wasn't it brave of her? And Papa will build another house and we shall all live in it together, and I expect you would be able to come too if you wished it, ma'am.'

Phyllida smiled to herself. It would take more than the ageing Henty to daunt Emma, it was clear.

As she went a little way up the drive, the wind whipped at her cloak, loosened her hair. Rain spattered upon her shoulders. But she felt neither the cold nor the wet, as she stood watching for Edward.

She saw him at last, coming through the thinning smoke. His face was streaked with grime. There were scorch marks on his clothes. He was without his hat and hair had come loose from its ribbon and was more untidy even than Kit's. Her heart contracted at sight of the lines of strain about his mouth and eyes. She longed to put her arms about him, smooth away all his cares.

He managed a smile as he reached her. 'The rain will do our work for us now. It will have more effect than the villagers' heroic efforts with a bucket chain from the river.'

She asked anxiously, 'Are they all safe—your servants?'

His smile broadened. 'Every one, thank God. And only the slightest of injuries—a few cuts from glass, a burn or two. They saved all the horses, too, and the dogs. It is only the house which has been . . .' He caught himself up. 'Forgive me, I should not have said that. It means so much to you. And I had planned it should be yours one day.'

She looked beyond him, to where 'Lady Sarah's house' was almost a shell. Red and yellow flames leaped spasmodically skywards, feeding on the charred timber. Soon the rain would damp them down. There would be nothing left but a reeking, smoking ruin. She gave an involuntary shudder.

Turning back to him, she put a hand on his arm. 'Do not think I am ungrateful. Kit told me about it. But—but I know now that this house could hold no happiness for me. Nor, I believe, for anyone else. It was built for a woman who killed herself because of her husband's cruelty. And now the wife of that woman's son, I understand, will have burned herself alive, in India, because he has abandoned her.' She looked searchingly into his face. 'I do not think you were really happy there, despite your lovely furnishings, your china and . . .'

'My dear Phyllida,' he said sadly. 'I do not expect to find much happiness anywhere.'

She lowered her eyes. 'Not even if you wish upon a lucky charm?' Drawing from her pocket the gold button from her riding suit, she held it out before him.

He drew in his breath, his eyes widened. 'Where did you find that?'

'Beside the rustic seat, where you left us.' She tilted up her chin, and tried to keep her voice serious. 'Mr. Glenister, I have made many false accusations against you. But I make one now which I know full well to be true. You are a thief.'

His smile was rueful. 'I admit it. Have you devised a fit punishment?'

'I think so.' She turned and walked a little away from him, to where an ornamental hedge hid her both from the wind and the eyes of onlookers. When he followed her, she said slowly, 'It is to tell you that all your plans for me have come to naught. "Lady Sarah's house" has gone, and I—I have no wish to marry Kit.'

He was silent for a moment before he asked, 'Why? Why this change?'

She faced him, looking straight into his eyes. 'Because, I think, I have at last grown up. My dreams were of childhood, as Kit was part of my childhood.'

His voice was very low. 'Are you sure? Little Phyllida, are you quite sure?'

'Yes,' she answered steadily. 'Kit has no need of me, you see. Neither had Francis Delaney, nor Uncle Samuel.'

'And you are seeking someone who does?'

'Do you know why I came here today? Because you told me that Emma missed me. And because . . .'

'Yes?' He bent his head towards her, she was speaking so softly.

'Because of Lord Clive.'

'Lord Clive?' he repeated, puzzled.

'I thought perhaps you might be in need of comfort, on that account. Was that so very foolish?'

He took her face between his hands. It did not matter to her that they were grimed with mud and blackened with soot.

'My dearest Phyllida, I would have dragged the very sun out of the sky for you, asking nothing from you in return, so deeply do I love you. But if you . . . If miracles can still happen, and you . . .' His voice broke. She saw that he was too moved to continue.

She covered his hands with her own. 'I do not deserve such love, Edward. But possessing it, I have all the world. If you think I can give you in return a little of the happiness I believe you have never known, you have only to ask me.'

His arms went round her. His lips on hers were gentle at first, tentative, reminding her of Kit's kisses. Then she no longer thought of Kit, or 'Lady Sarah's house'. Or even Emma, who would be her daughter. She knew at last just how false had been her dreams. Real love, and all of the future joy were now embodied in this man who held her tightly in his arms and who was kissing her in a way that was no longer gentle.